Train
River
Short
Stories

2020

DEDICATION

This book is dedicated
to every writer who has dared
to share their story.

Contents

FOREWARD

Welcome to our first collection of short stories. It has been an incredible honor to read and explore the hundreds of short stories that were submitted for consideration. We are so excited to share our favorites with you.

Inside you'll find stories about love, life, death, and heartbreak. Stories that inspire reverence, fear, sympathy and delight.

The factor that unites these stories is their resonance. Each story in this edition grabbed our imagination and held tight. These are the stories that sink into our subconscious and reemerge in moments of quiet, begging for reexamination.

We hope you'll enjoy exploring these stories as much as we have.

Love always,

Train River Publishing

Thank You

We would like to extend a special thank you to our incredible Supporting Members who make our publications possible. With their support we have been able to build incredible contemporary anthologies.

SUPPORTING MEMBERS

Eileen Wiscombe
Annie Percik
Jenni Jolly
Lana Hechtman Ayers
Lauren Michelle
Stephanie Robertson
Sian Maciejowski
William Falo
Marcia Knight-Latter
Karl Kadie
Elizabeth
KC
Jessica
Anonymous

Barbara Soehner
Tanja Krstulovic
Jessica Bullard
Amelia Robyn
James Goggin
thewhite.m05
Joan Gerstein
CEC Haydon
Sam Piscitelli
Leon Gregori
Dakota Avellino
Marie Claire
TazThePoet

We look forward to continuing to grow and publish more poets and authors. Thank you for joining us on this journey.

2020

KATLYN MINARD

Death in a Hollywood Edit Bay

SHE CHOKED. THAT'S what they told us.

They found her in the morning: sitting stiff in her swivel chair before a trio of glowing monitors, her back flush against the mesh netting, as if her own fine edit had totally blown her away. Feet flexed and L-shaped. Converse toe caps pointed heavenward. Fish-white hands frozen claw-like at her collarbone. Her lips were still puckered, her arctic eyes still wide with astonishment, like a teen girl reeling from a fierce first kiss.

It happened while she was working late — hours after the rest of us had gone home to packed bongs and hard spouses in soft beds. Nobody was around to hear if she banged on the walls, or hurled herself against the edge of her desk. Maybe she reached for the door handle, groped blindly for it with one hand while the other hand clutched at her rapidly closing airway. Maybe not. Editors always work with the door closed. We'll never know for sure.

What do we know for sure?

Thirteen hours.

1

That's how long she sat soulless in our workplace, staring teary-eyed up into the fluorescent lights and blasting air vent, while we dreamed in the dark with our eyes closed.

And we know what she choked on.

Chicken.

Specifically, sweet and sour chicken.

We know this because of the coroner's report, but mainly because of the sauce.

It's still there — hiding in the crevices of her vinyl work desk. Little lines of orange slime, somehow still sticky after rounds and rounds of disinfectant. She must have spilled it during the struggle. A pocket-creased receipt confirmed she ordered the takeout from Ming Dragon: a shadowy dive on Sunset frequented by post-production paper pushers. Inside, framed glamour shots of dead superstars covered the walls. Selena. Marilyn. MJ. All behind glass. Nothing transforms a human into a saint like an untimely death.

I remember chatting with her there once, over a late lunch. Between spring rolls, I griped about my growing entry-level boredom. It was starting to seem impossible to get noticed and rise up, even after two years of tireless transcribing, footage-finding, and boot-licking — my monotonous Red Queen's Race.

"Don't worry, it'll happen," she reassured me as she dunked her chicken in sweet 'n' sour, "just be patient. Keep busting your ass. And the promotion will come. It always does, eventually."

Lamest. Advice. Ever. I could've found something equally profound tucked into the corners of my unwrapped fortune cookie. At that point I tapped my chopsticks on my plate, the way you tap your foot when you've been waiting in line for eternity. "How eventually?"

She shrugged her delicate shoulders. "In my experience," she replied, "usually when you least expect it. When you feel like you're at the end of your rope."

Her funeral fell on a Friday. An army of black-suited mourners under a brilliant blue sky.

During the eulogy I watched the palm trees sway against each other in the breeze like stoned beach bums. I listened to the slow creak of the lowering coffin, drowned out by chirping birds. It seemed inappropriate and gauche to hold such a grim event on such a glorious day. But it couldn't be helped. In Los Angeles, nothing is certain except death, and ludicrously perfect weather.

My boss must have felt inappropriate too. He waited until the service concluded to corner me on the sidewalk. He spoke like a kid at a pharmacy counter buying his first box of condoms: desperate eyes downcast, shoulders hunched, voice hushed in embarrassment.

"We're still on a deadline." He rubbed the bridge of his nose. "How would you feel about starting Monday?"

It's a long walk today, from my cubicle to her edit bay.

The other editors I pass all see me in the reflection of their monitors and turn to look. They work with their doors open now.

But I won't.

As soon as my boss feels comfortable leaving me alone, I quietly close the door behind me.

The monitors are dark. The post-it notes once plastered to its corners have been peeled off. The desk reeks of Lysol. A work station wiped clean of its worker. Even though this bay is all prepped and sanitized for my first official morning as an editor, I can't bring myself to unpack my things right away. This still feels like her space. The only thing I unpack is my breakfast: a baggie of dry frosted mini wheats. No milk. We don't need another spill.

Once I'm in the swivel chair, it's surprising how easily I lapse right back into work mode. There's a lot to do today. Address the fine cut notes, fix the first act, compress the final act, pick up everywhere she left off...this may be a work-through-lunch kind of day. Maybe I'll just order takeout.

I lay my palm on the mouse to log into the computer. My wrist rests on the edge of the desk and when I pick it up, it comes away sticky. Slashed with slime. A witchy little vein in the belly of my arm, from that sweet meat that turned everything sour.

The sight of my arm under these fluorescents hits a nerve, and for the briefest of moments my body feels like it's back at the plasma center in Van Nuys. I spent many gloomy nights there in my first LA months, selling my blood plasma for grocery money. I used to sit in that long leather chair — digging my fingers into a smiley-shaped stress ball as mechanical monsters slurped the plasma from my veins — wondering when the universe would cut me a break.

Maybe it finally did.

Maybe it led me from that chair...all the way into this one.

She was right, that day at lunch. She was right all along. Only the promotion didn't come at the end of my rope.

It came at the end of hers.

LUCY GARDNER

When the Storm Ends

WHEN I WAS NINE, I watched my Dad fall from a two-story roof. It was awkward and slow, and I was paralyzed and worthless in my existence. I just stood there, barefoot on the gravel in my dirty shorts and t-shirt. I stood there in the same gravel that broke his fall and fractured his spine. I stood there as his workers ran up to him in a panic as he laid there in agony. Wailing like a little child. I stood there like I'd never seen him cry before. Because I hadn't.

Dad and I both acquired a new fear that day. A new weakness. His was heights. Mine was him. I find it impressive that he still continues to climb ladders, scale steep roofs, and scare me into unnervingly deep anxieties that I doubt I'll ever shake. His doctor calls him a crazy bastard. I beg him not to roof the houses he works on anymore, but he says it costs too much money to hire another hand. After his trembling legs caused another accident, not as big as the first, he caved to my demands of harnessing himself to the roof. The harness I bought from the hardware store has an anchor that attaches itself to the ridge of the roof, strapping the roofer in a mass of bands like a rock climber.

"I am not wearing goddamn suspenders on the roof," Dad said as I tore them from the bag.

"You will unless you're okay with never speaking to me again," I said. He stared at me then at the harness, took a gruff sigh, grabbed the harness from my hand and left. The next day at work, he wore the harness and swore if anyone mentioned it, he'd throw them off the roof himself. The new kid my dad hired smirked then turned away as his mouth widened into a crooked toothy smile. I smiled too, but I'm not sure if it was at my Dad's comment or the new kid's ridiculous grin.

There's extra help needed on the job today, so I get to work with the new kid. Dad says his name is Hank. My curiosity piqued, I get ready for the day with a vigor that is unusual for a workday. Dad doesn't let me come on days when his "workin' boys" are there. When I get to the site, I reach the room where Dad is by following his loud nail-gun pops. The pops echo through the empty house like firecrackers.

"Hey," I scream over the nail-gun. Dad stops and turns around. Johnny Cash bellows through the radio on the floor. Hank turns around too, still holding a sheet of drywall in place for Dad to nail it up.

"Hey," Hank says. His dark hair looks unbrushed, and his right cheek protrudes like he's been to the dentist. My dad looks from Hank to me then says I'm taking his spot next to Hank for the day. Dad turns back to nail up the sheet. Hank's arm never wavered while holding it. Then Dad climbs down his step ladder, hands me the nail-gun, and walks out to assign the others. Happy with my assignment, I climb the ladder without comment. Hank says nothing as we continue the job.

In the next room, I ask Hank if he wants to switch places. He'll nail; I'll lift. I wait for a sucking of teeth or a laugh, but he just nods and grabs the gun. He hums along to the radio as he nails up my sheets. I work in rhythmic pain, denying my arms the relief they need from the weight of the drywall.

I forget the pain when I realize Hank's nail-gun pops have quieted. I look up and he's sitting on a ladder rung, hunched over and eerily white. He slithers his body to the floor like the ladder morphed into a slide, and I see blood dripping. He impaled himself with a nail. Body stiff, he looks at me, and I stare back waiting for him to cry or curse or pretend like he didn't do it. Finally he holds his skewered hand up to his eyes. He examines it like a magic trick. One he needs the explanation for but doesn't have. My impatience with his examination climaxes, so I squat to look him in the eyes which shock me with color; I grab his hand, yank the nail out the way it went through him, and drop it beside him. Bloody and crooked at the end, it stayed there as evidence of our first encounter for the rest of the week. The homeowner who hired Dad for the remodel accused us of murdering her missing cat with it.

After the nail incident, we continue to schedule days where we work together. We mostly work in silence, and the tenseness that usually stems from silence with a stranger never manifests in our time together. I drown in my introversion, and he jails himself in his. I paint; he paints. He lifts the drywall; I nail it up. He trips over tools; I laugh. He never questions my abilities or makes the inappropriate comments that usually come from Dad's workin' boys. About my legs, hips, hair. I am his equal.

He chews tobacco though. It's always stuck in his cheek like he needs it for hibernation. The spaces between his teeth blacken sometimes and I gag dramatically to show my disgust.

"Hey, it's not so bad if you'd try it," he says with a laugh.

"You're kidding."

7

"Nah, all my buddies chew. And my old girlfriend did." The last part, he says with finality like his ex-girlfriend should be what changes my mind.

"Your old girlfriend won't have any teeth in ten years."

"Neither will I, I reckon." I don't say anything back and decide to repaint what I just rolled.

"Your Dad doesn't like that I chew, does he?" he says, deciding to continue. Still sitting on the floor with our trash from lunch, he looks comfortable and slightly amused. Kind of how people look after three beers.

"Why do you care what my Dad thinks?" I say. He laughs and moves to get up.

Without looking at me, he says, "I just know you'd never be with anyone like me because he wouldn't let you." He looks back and his expression is more serious now. Silenced with his playful jab, I know he's right. It's why Dad lets me work with Hank. He knows I'd never want him.

"My dad doesn't dictate who I date," I say.

"Then let's go out," he says, "tonight." Excitement and alarm flush me with heat.

"Where would we go?"

"I know a place you'd like. You just have to trust me." He smiles at me with all of his crooked endearment. His eyes are light. I catch a glimpse of Dad walking around with a board through the window behind Hank. He'd never think I'd say yes.

"Okay," I say. "No chewing though." He laughs and nods then drops the paintbrush he held in the floor, scaring the dirty hardwood.

Later that night, I shower and get ready to go. Suddenly conscious of how I look, I rip through my drawers of clothes, irritated with the lack of stylish choices. I curse at myself for caring about it and slip on my most comfortable pair of jeans and a t-shirt. It's just Hank, I remind myself. I hear his '79 Ford pickup roar it's warning as it pulls in the driveway. He's early. My pulse pounds through my temple. Dad is still home. And he doesn't know about the date. I run lightly across the house, so as to appear in the kitchen with Dad nonchalantly. He's sitting at the table squinting at his calculator. "Hey Dad, I'm going out," I say. "I'll see you tonight."

I'm not fast enough. The doorbell rings and Hank is peering through the glass door. Dad looks at Hank then at me. Confusion masks his face. Then recognition. Then anger. His mouth is tight.

"You gonna answer that?" Dad says, motioning to Hank. I walk over and open the door. Hank's eyes shoot daggers at mine. He watched us through the glass.

"Hey," I say. He doesn't say anything back. His face is unreadable and he no longer looks at me. I notice he looks different than usual. His hair is combed down, and his eyes appear dark in the dimness of the room. They complement the black collared shirt he put on. Still wearing beaten jeans and his work boots, he looks ruggedly handsome.

Realizing no one intends on breaking the silence for me, I say, "Dad, I'm going out with Hank like I said. We'll see you later." My words come out choked and broken like the moment.

"No," he says. "You're not."

"Why," I say. A rush of anger heats my neck. I feel Hank's presence stiffen beside me.

"Go on home, Hank," Dad says. Hank turns his head to look at me. His face is calm. Like he was expecting a storm all along. I'd never felt moved to hold him until now.

As Hank moves to pass me out the door, I grab his arm. "I'm coming." His lips part like he might speak, but he doesn't. He nods. Reddened now, my dad's face glows with the contrast of his blue eyes. They too, glow with emotion. It hurts to see him hurt. Knowing I've made my decision, Dad says nothing else and turns to leave the room. I shut the door behind me.

"You didn't have to do that for me," he said as we climb in the truck.

"Yes, I did," I say. He drives onto the main road, and I see him hide a smile as he looks out his driver's window. "So where are we going?" I say.

"You'll see," he says with his usual playfulness. I decide to give up and let him take me away. A heaviness leaves me, and I lean back and let the swaying of his driving drunken me. The town roads eventually morph to country dirt ones, and the trees surrounding us grow taller and wider, oscillating shadows along the road before us. When we pull to a stop, a creek breaks the woody landscape of forest around us. The bank that Hank pulled onto with his truck is sandy and wide. His tires sink and we sit unevenly balanced now. Weeping willows grace the scene with their sadness, tangled branches hanging down into the water. Broken pines lay split across the creek from a storm. Animals have adopted new homes in them.

"How did you find this?" I lean into his dash to see more.

"This was my parents' land when I was a kid. I used to play here all the time."

"Can we get out?" I ask, then I feel self-conscious about my childish amazement.

"I thought you'd never ask," he says with his goofy grin. I follow him down to the water and across the rocks he hops to make it to the other side. My left shoe screams with suffocation after I slip and get creek water inside. The squishing sound gives me away, and Hank laughs. After dodging some tree branches and picking through briars, we make it past enough brush to see a quarry built with boulders and rocks from the creek. "This used to be a dam when I was a kid, but it got blown out with a flash flood. This was my favorite place in the world. My only place to get away, ya know?"

"Yeah, it's beautiful. I didn't know you liked stuff like this," I say. He grins.

"Yeah, there's a lot you don't know about me."

When I get home, the lights are off and Dad is asleep early. It feels lonely when it's quiet, only me and Dad to fill the space. I feel surprisingly light tonight though. I talked more with Hank at the creek than I've talked with anyone in a long time. And it felt so good. So at home.

Every day I spend with Hank now grows me in my affections for him. However, Dad speaks to me sparingly. He tells me when he needs me at work. He asks what I need from the grocery store. And he grunts back when I say goodnight. Our silence at the dinner table is excruciating. My throat burns with anger and hurt. His silence speaks it. Apart from this distance, he still lets Hank work for him. And he allows him to pick me up at night with no protests. He even gives the occasional nod to Hank. That nod is my hope.

Dad and Hank roof the Kirks' house today, and although I have protested work because of the coming weather, both men surprisingly agree to ignore my objections. As promised, I made my way to the Kirks' to oversee the job after school. The sky, already dark and brooding, rumbles its warnings as I pull in the drive. Dad and Hank are on the roof now, Hank at the ridge and Dad handing up shingles. Rain sprinkles my face as I climb out of my car.

"Hey," I shout, "That's enough for today." They look down at me. Hank smiles as his hair blows around on his head.

Dad says, "We're not done yet." The rain is harder now. Trees are leaning and waving and snapping.

"Dad, I'm serious. This is ridiculous." I look around for support, but Dad's other workers have retreated to their homes for the day.

"I don't want the water getting in the house. We're almost done." He says it sternly without looking. Frustration rumbles in me like the storm. Then I see it. As

11

though he isn't being difficult enough, Dad isn't wearing the harness. The worst day to not wear it, he didn't. I squint to make sure, and I see him shaking as he balances in place still handing Hank the slabs of shingles. Adrenaline rushes through me as I run to Dad's truck to retrieve the harness. I open the toolbox on the back, rip it from the mass of equipment he has stashed in the compartment, and run to climb the ladder to the roof. Hank is yelling now, but it's muffled by the wind. Water sheaths my view as it thickens the sky, and my hair sticks to my face. I climb the ladder's rungs and slip twice but catch myself.

When I reach the top, Hank and Dad move towards me. They've finally given up. The space between us seems vast with a sheet of rain as a divider. They crouch into the storm and move slowly across the roof. Hank shields his eyes from the rain with a hand. Dad holds his out beside him to balance. He still wobbles. I stand stationary on the ladder, focused on their movements like I can will them to move how I need them to. The harness, pointless now, hangs from my hand. I let it drop.

Wind force pushes the trees surrounding the house into a bend like they've been brushed with a comb. The ladder I stand on wavers for a moment as though it might topple. My weight means nothing to mother nature. A gust rips through the air, and I feel the ladder lift again. I grab the gutter next to me. A thud vibrates my hand. I look up and Dad is clinging to the eave of the roof, half of his body dangling over concrete. Twice as big as Hank, Dad's body snaps the gutter supporting him. Hank is feet above him, laying across the ridge to fight being thrown off himself.

A wave of adrenaline makes my vision fuzzy. I climb over the roof's edge and jump to grab the ridge too. The roof is steep and too slick to cross now without a grip. I run sideways down the length of the roof, gripping the ridge and twisting my ankle. I can't feel that foot now. The gutter Dad is on finally caves under his weight and it drops two-stories onto the concrete. Dad hangs with dead weight by his fingers. I scream at Hank to help, but he only looks at me, his black hair painting his forehead above wide eyes.

"Help me," I scream, tears crowding my vision. Trembling, he moves towards me. We slide down to the eave where Dad is trying to hoist himself over.

"I'm just gonna jump down," Dad says, almost breathless. He looks at me full in the face for the first time since Hank picked me up that night. "You two need to get down safely."

"Wait," I say, grabbing his left arm. "We can get you up." Tree branches bound across the roof now. One flies over our heads by a foot. Hank moves to grab Dad's other arm, then slips. Almost comically, Hank's feet slipped out from under him, and his back caught the roof's shingles. He toppled the edge awkwardly like he tried to avoid hitting Dad. Grabbing at the air with two hands, he catches the roof with one. Dad lets go with one hand and fumbles to catch Hank from falling. Then he falls.

I'm silenced with shock as I watch Dad hit the ground. He tried to land on his feet, and he did, but only for a moment. He's lying on the ground now, still and disfigured. Hank still hangs in front of me, screaming. I pause and look at Hank before moving. He's crying. I grab his hand and yank him hard as he slings the rest of his body over. We jump up to grab the ridge again and edge towards the ladder. I go first and without looking behind me, I move forward until I see Dad. I run towards him in panic. I see movement, and I'm livened again.

As I move closer, I see bone. And blood. Red hellish blood. Covered in busted tendons and red muscle, the bone breathes air for the first time. Ripped open at the knee, the tibia shot out from the impact of falling feet-first. I crouch at his head and hold it as he stares up at nothing. I put my hand on his chest to feel the beat. Hank screams into his

13

phone.

Weeks later, Dad laughs as I doodle on his cast. I hope
it'll take away from the attention his walker gets. "I'm a
true old man now," he says, glaring at the walker.

"You won't always need that," I say. He nods with a tight
smile.

"We'll see." After he sips his coffee, he asks, "You talked
to Hank lately?"

"No."

"Why not?" I shake my head and draw a sunshine. "None
of that was his fault, you know," Dad says, looking down at
my marker.

"I know."

LISA MARIE LOPEZ

The Flowers that Changed Him

I OFFERED RUSTY MY LAST 7-UP as we began our walk
home from Burger Haven. Work had been miserable and
Rusty was trudging through the parking lot like a crazy
man, fists clenched and all. Before long, he was on to his
weekly rants: out-of-order vending machines, stove knobs
that wouldn't turn, and of course, the customers that made
his life impossible. I added my own two cents about the
doorless restroom stall, and that's when we stumbled upon
a cluster of yellow flowers lying on the roadside.

Tied together with pink ribbon, we realized they had
been placed there in remembrance of somebody. Rusty
crouched in the dirt, carefully reassembling the flowers.
Several had loosened from the ribbon. He took his time,
gathering rocks and twigs, trying to keep everything in
place. I stood beside him, directing traffic. He didn't utter
a single word the entire time. I had never seen Rusty work
with such pride and attention to detail. If only he'd work
half this hard at the Haven, he could earn himself a plaque
for Employee of the Month. I'd been given one two months
before. Rusty liked teasing me about it, calling me
September's Golden Boy, or Prestigious Paul.

For the remainder of our walk home, Rusty didn't say all but one word. When we reached Sherwood Avenue, I shook his hand and told him to get good rest. Tomorrow was Double Deal Tuesday at Burger Haven. Noon would be a mad house, the line most likely snaking out the door.

Rusty said he'd be there early. He wanted to make sure there were plenty of little ketchup and mustard packets on hand. He wanted to make sure the food was fresh, and the tables shined.

Sketching

AS FAR AS WE KNEW, Aunt Nancy was our only living relative and when we were small children my sister and I were taken to live with her. We never saw our parents again.

It was during the late nineteen sixties, the time when eccentricity began to be accepted as normal. This other-world type of reasoning must have suited Aunt Nancy. The world swung wild with colour and free love, and though flower power figured high on her choice of homemade clothing, as a spinster, I suspect free love was something she only ever read about in old newspapers. She survived on a meagre living as a seamstress and made most of our clothes. The material came from whatever she saved from her work. This often resulted in us looking like twins with matching patchwork dresses. My younger sister, Sarah was happy about that but I always wanted better.

Whilst femininity sparkled through her our aunt's blue, smiling eyes it did not radiate through her demeanour. Elegance was not her greatest feature. Tall, with an ungainly walk, arms flapping in uncoordinated intent, her frame resembled a butterfly in a gale, imbalanced by the draughts on its wings. Her head would push forward, alert as if seeking out some secret food store to supplement our echoing larder. Between her fingers, would be a hand rolled cigarette while behind her trailed the confused scents of tobacco smoke and gardenia perfume in a discarded swirl. Beneath her fur coat were bright coloured skirts with small pebbles sewn into the hems so they flew around her ankles like adoring pets. Sitting on the back of her head was always a scarlet beret hat-pinned on with two white seagull feathers to contrast with the dark brown hair curling over her shoulders.

I cannot ever remember her wanting any more than she had. If one of us ever asked for something seemingly attainable she would wave her long arms as if to brush it from our mind as an unnecessary or useless item. Content with her life, she expected nothing more so was not disappointed by its inadequacies. For my part, as a child who did want more, her attitude mystified me.

Family photographs were kept in a huge album under the stairs. Aunt Nancy was my mother's sister and, from the pictures we saw they were strikingly similar. When she told us about them growing up together they also seemed alike in personality. As teenagers, they would dress up in fairy costumes to walk along the beach collecting shells and seaweed. Sarah too possessed this family resemblance and though not as inelegant, had our aunt's same instinctive way of looking at life from odd angles. I would often hear them discuss the mysteries of plant growth, or cheese or some other subject normally taken for granted. She was not only a parent but also a mentor encouraging us to use imagination in every area of life.

Our treat was visiting her favourite place, the local cemetery. If the weather permitted we would walk there most weekends. The three of us would sit on a crypt near the church to share a flask of tea and a large bundle of plum jam sandwiches. During birthdays an occasional packet of custard creams might appear. Sarah and I regarded those days as special times. We had few luxuries but for her love.

On one occasion Aunt Nancy found a man lying on his back on a partially caved in grave. His leg had gone down through the earth causing him to fall backwards onto the cavity. He lay still, clutching a bunch of orange dahlias to his chest. She stood watching him for ages. She told us she wished she could have left him there. It was the only time I heard her say she wished for something. 'He looked so peaceful,' she said, 'like an angel in his duffle coat and wellingtons.' But each time he moved, more soil fell in and she wondered if the whole grave might fall in, taking him with it. He asked if she would mind helping him up - please? Being a lady of impeccable etiquette she always accentuated his "please" when reciting the story. In her opinion, if it must be a choice between money and manners then wealth would be a sad substitute for courtesy. However, from my view of the world, money had the ability to bring much more happiness than the little courtesies of life could.

When upright, the man thanked her and after brushing down his coat he gave her the orange dahlias then left. She never forgot him. And, would always point out the grave, telling us, with a smile how, every time he struggled more earth fell in. I think she kept returning in the hope she would find him lying there again. She never did.

Aunt Nancy could look at things as though she had never seen them before, marveling at clouds, odd shaped stones, even chairs or phone boxes. Once she made us pick up a dandelion each and hug it till the petals squashed flat. 'They will come back to us,' she would say. 'Love is hope.' But she never found love and we never knew what she hoped for. Unless it was to find the man lying on the grave again.

She taught us rope pulling sequences for bell ringing. Our small trio would stand together waiting to pull on her command. Aunt Nancy had two ropes, Sarah and I had a rope each. We would practice the routines for ten minutes every Wednesday evening after tea, ready for Sunday service. She believed this to be good exercise for disciplined musical instruction. But as the church bells had long been sold to help pay for a new oak door, we had to imagine the sounds. I never could manage to do this, but she and Sarah would shut their eyes to drift entranced into their own music. Though she had no definite religious beliefs, on Sundays we went to church early to pull the ropes before the service. And as we pulled, we would each have to shout 'ding' or 'dong' to imply credibility.

Later, in the cemetery she would lay posing on the graves, her inelegance smoothed out by her prostrate position. She would tell us to watch from a short distance and ask us how she looked. Should she adjust her body or lean her head to one side to improve the artistic influence? Was she portraying angelic protection for the deceased beneath her? On the taller, ornamental sculptures her body would be wrapped around the stone in various Hollywood poses for our opinions on the effect. Was her chin held high enough? Should she drape an arm, or let the cigarette hang loose from her lips? However, when finished, she always showed respect to those incumbent, thanking them with a theatrical bow.

As she posed I would make quick, rough sketches of her in an exercise book. But I could never complete one to any degree of satisfaction. She would flit from one grave to another like some mischievous cherub trying to avoid salvation. I had books full of drawings I never felt happy with because they were too rushed. No matter how I tried to finish them later they never gave me any sense of fulfillment. I could never capture the magic I felt inside as when the pencil initially sped across my page.

At home we would go through the sketches and she would try to perfect the poses again on our old, chintz sofa. But the moments of enchantment were gone, left with the dead and the stonework. Maybe their stillness accentuated the aura glowing around her. Some sketches she would like enough to cut from the book then pin it to the inside of the food cupboard door. There were no pictures on show in the house. They would be hidden away in drawers or boxes. Pictures were of the past, she would say. She lived in the present.

At eighteen I went to university. With a degree in architecture I took a job in London. It was demanding work but, determined to find the success I always wanted I pushed myself hard. Not long after I left home Sarah married and soon had two children. She stayed living in the house, taking it over when our aunt died. We buried her in the cemetery she loved. At her graveside we sat with flasks of tea, jam sandwiches and biscuits. It was a day of sad celebration for a beautiful person.

Life exerts its pressures and my visits were not regular. We kept in touch mainly by greetings cards and phone calls. Twenty years later I moved back nearer to my old home and took up sketching again. I joined a life drawing class in the local community hall. About ten of us collected in a soulless, magnolia room under neon lighting. The model reclined on her side atop a long centre table. Being the last to enter I had to sit behind her to sketch.

Streaks of long greying hair weaved between the mousy browns that fell past her shoulders. I followed the curve of her spine as her arm leaned on a pile of cushions. She was not a young woman, but similar in height and build to Aunt Nancy, slightly overweight, sagging around the buttocks and lumpy thighs. But she was a living model and my mind buzzed with exhilaration at the prospect of drawing her without the constant interruption I had been used to. The woman was everything I imagined my aunt to be and I immersed myself in her shape and the rush of HB graphite on paper.

21

For everyone to have an equal view the group changed seating positions. I therefore drew two pictures, one from the back and another from the front. She was a delight to draw. I stared far too long at the contours of her body. Her breasts drooped as they should at her age and her belly hung a little too low. Flesh folded across her thighs in hard shadows under the strip lights and I relished smudging out these lines into soft, pale shades.

I did not look at her face. It was not necessary. I was drawing Aunt Nancy and I could remember every inch of her from the neck up, the rounded chin, full cheeks, slightly humped nose, wide forehead and those eager, searching eyes. To see the model's face would have ruined my illusion.

I searched for a frame to hold the frontal drawing and display it at its best. I wanted a showpiece to prove to myself I finally had what I yearned for. I found the one I wanted in an up-market antique shop. Light oak set with a thin silver inlay and narrow mount, it hung above the fireplace. I would sit staring at it imagining being with her again running through the cemetery, grasping at the pose, flinging over the page to catch her next position. I felt her presence with me again and my aspiration was complete. But there was still something missing. The picture wanted more from me. She wanted more.

I took it down and removed it from the frame. I had my drawing. It was all I wanted, without fuss or embellishment. Now it is pinned to the inside of the food cupboard door where she would have wanted it. I gaze at it every day as I eat my plum jam sandwich. Sometimes I light a gardenia scented candle.

The End

For the Joy of Panda Tiles

CLARA STARED at the black and white tiles on the restaurant bathroom floor. If you looked at it the right way the tiles formed pandas. Larger white octagons were the head and body with smaller black tiles at the sides, creating ears, hands and feet or paws, Clara knew that was the right word. Once she had called her toes, foot fingers and her mother and father hadn't stopped laughing about it all through dinner. Eating at the restaurant was better than eating at home. The meat her mother cooked curled up hard and everything else, the mash potatoes out of the box and the frozen vegetables were too soft and soggy. Dinner at the Wedgewood was something else entirely.

She waited with her parents under the tapestry that depicted a medieval hunting scene for their turn at the cafeteria counter. Mack, Clara's favorite waiter, was there ready to dish out her roast chicken, real mash potatoes and string beans. He smiled at her from behind the steaming trays of golden chicken gravy the same color as his uniform jacket.

At the table Clara's parents talked and talked not like the other adults sitting alone together staring off in different directions slowly lifting their forks to their empty lips. Clara's mother spoke quickly. She shot her sentences off like rubber bands. Snap! Her father's voice was low and he spoke slowly as if he was giving you time to catch on. When Clara had scraped the last of her chocolate mousse into her spoon and gobbled it up she headed off to see the pandas.

The bathroom was her favorite part of any restaurant but the Wedgewood's was especially cozy. There was a little room when you walked in that had a thick carpet of swirling flowers. Along one whole wall was a mirror that was tinted just dark enough, Clara noticed, to make you look more like yourself. She would sit on her knees propped up on the pink cushioned stools and stare at her reflection and wait for other guests to come through the heavy wooden door.

When ladies came in they would smile at her and sometimes have a bit of a chat about how good the food was or what a nice tan she had. Her mother had put her dark hair in a pony tail on top of her head. Clara liked to pull it out like the top of a pineapple. I want to be a bathroom attendant when I grow up she would tell anyone who would listen. Ambitious, isn't she? Her mother would say.

Even if Clara didn't need to use the toilet she liked to sit on the cold whiteness and look at the happy pandas. I could stay here forever, she thought and when she did that cartwheel off the curb right into the path of the #66 bus that's just where she flew – right back to her pandas, in heaven, now, Clara surmised.

The Crater

WE HUDDLED TOGETHER in the dusty crater. The barren earth pushed between my toes and through my fingers as I ran my hands up and down in the empty space beside me. No one spoke much. The odd comment here and there but as if only to remember the sound of our voices.

There were not many of us in the crater now. I think eight remained. But I cannot rely on the memory.

We had existed amongst darkness for as long as I could remember. Few stars remained visible, but the moon hung lower in the sky, casting a foreboding, yet familiar glow over our features. I remained in a state of both consciousness and unconsciousness, not in the space between. And we did not sleep anymore, although never were we truly awake.

It was not just us. We were more sure of that than anything else. But when one of our group had left the crater to confirm our only truth, they did not come back. We knew it was not because they had found others. After spending what seemed to be an infinite length of time amongst the same bodies, you knew when they had stopped breathing. The air would become thicker. The difference almost imperceptible, but you could feel the added weight on your chest. Yet to us, the implication of this thickened air was not sinister. It was purely an observation, the same as seeing the blackness replace another star.

Just another step.

I was not sure for how long I had been running my fingers through the dirt, but I saw that it had pushed under my fingernails and they bled. I became fascinated with the dirt invading my body and began to scratch the soil with fervour. No one took notice of my heightened movements. These flickers in behaviour were not out of the ordinary anymore.

When I was satisfied with the depth I had created, validated by the blood-dampened soil, I moved on to the space in front. I resumed with the same urgency. The others around me were replaced by the blackness and they faded into the sky.

The linearity of time was a redundant notion, so I cannot be sure for how long the digging and bleeding took place. All I can say is that I continued digging until I did not.

I stopped.

My raw fingers had reached a layer that was not soil. I inspected the hole before me, but the darkness must have dripped in and saturated the empty space when I was not looking. I continued to blindly feel out the subterranean layer, relying solely on my desensitised fingers to compose an image in my mind. After being enveloped in grit and distortion for so long, my consciousness and unconsciousness were, for some time, not able to find a word to explain the surface beneath my fingers. (Again, it would be wrong to assign a measure of time to my dualistic disconnect. I use the term 'some time' colloquially. Merely a hangover from the errors of the past world.)

It was smooth. The surface was smooth. And cold, despite its deep suppression in the soil. I let my fingers adjust to these distant sensations and allowed a more coherent image to form.

It was not a layer. It was an object. I could feel the curved edges.

I pulled more dirt away from these edges until my fingers hooked around each side. I needed to uproot the object from the dripping darkness to examine it in the moonlight. It began to loosen from its bed and I raised it towards me with precaution. It was much heavier than I had anticipated. Denser than any object I could remember handling. As it rose, the moonlight revealed effulgent scatterings across its surface. Or perhaps the light was emanating from within the object. They were clustered like microcosmic constellations and their radiance ebbed and flowed in harmony with my breath.

It was large and elliptical in shape. At first glance, the backdrop of the constellations was as black as the hole from which it had been born, but I soon saw a purple iridescence rippling over the darkness and beneath the stars.

It was beautiful.

I began to trace my hands across the surface and beneath the sides.

I stopped.

Under the right edge, the smooth surface was interrupted with a small indentation. Too well-defined to be a natural crack. Too perfect to be man-made. The incongruity of the deliberate indent against the smoothness held significance and the object suddenly felt heavier in my hands. I was fixated. I delicately hooked my index finger into the indentation and the object responded instantly, clicking out a small part of itself. As if I had flicked on a switch. But no light appeared. I had only aggravated the darkness.

The sound around me dampened, leaving behind a tinnital white noise, the noise heard just before passing into unconsciousness. The group slowly turned their heads towards me in harmony. So it wasn't just in my head. This object, as beautiful as it was terrible, had pried open the monotonous safety of our crater.

The piercing ringing crescendoed and crescendoed until suddenly--nothing. An abyss of silence. And that's when it started. It began so faintly, but layered over nothingness, its volume was deafening. A steady ticking. Yet to my surprise it was not coming from the object, rather it permeated through the dystopian world around us, through the air that we were breathing. I started to feel something I could not remember feeling and I could see that the others felt it too.

Fear. Pure, crippling fear. A fear abated only by an apathetic resignation to the inevitable.

Emotions and physical responses that had been lost and forgotten were suddenly surging through my body, through my blood.

The ticking was getting louder.

I looked at the group and their expressive faces as if I was seeing them for the first time. I felt recognition and warmth towards them and I was scared for them too. I turned to my left and recognised the face of my sister. We must have been together in the crater this whole time. I wanted to protect her, to protect us, but I knew we had reached the end. I wished I had seen her sooner.

Louder still.

We held stares and our eyes were damp. I grabbed her hand and the warmth of her touch ignited even more unnamed responses within me. I wanted to run, to get out of this crater, to be with her before.

Louder. Louder.

We fled the crater, shaking hand in shaking hand, in search of some place. Not safe. We knew now that nowhere was safe, but at the very least some place that we could hide beneath a shelter of both denial and acceptance, that this was finally it.

Our solace of eternal limbo had been torn out from under us with the flick of a switch and for the first time in my life, I could feel and apprehend my own impending mortality. I understood both life and death and the in between. The alluring futility of it all.

We ran barefoot across the soil and grit until we reached a small, cavernous space we could fill. We knelt down with our heads between our muddy knees, my sister's hand still in mine, damp eyes clamped shut, the other hand over the exposed ear. It proved hopeless in dampening the omnipresent, all-consuming ticking, but fear had reverted us back to our basal biological reflexes. I could feel the pounding of my blood in every inch of my body.

This was it.

The thick, damp air inside our rocky opening became lighter. I did not have the courage to open my eyes, they were now closed indefinitely, but I could feel the rock formations lifting above us. Gravity must have been the next victim to be drawn upwards into the darkness. I gripped tighter on my sister's hand so that we would be together when it happened. I gripped so tightly that I forced more blood from my fingernails onto hers.

Emptiness crept slowly into the space between our folded knees and the dirt beneath them. We were relinquished from the burden of our futile fears. They escaped through arched backs in gravity's wake. We were weightless. Devoid of all irrational preconceptions of our existence. And we were no longer scared.

The ticking continued relentlessly until climaxing into a cacophonous thunder. It fulminated in the distance and rolled towards us in a mounting wave through the weightless air. Drowning everything in its path.

And then heat.

Heat like I had never experienced before consumed my body. I did not feel pain. The last drops of blood from my fingernails, still digging into my sister's hand, were sucked into the darkness.

Tiny God

THEY MOVE INTO MY HOUSE for a short while. They bring with them their clothes and books, their toiletries, memories, and knick-knacks. They bring with them their tiny god.

When they arrive, the Duke greets me with warm hugs and a grateful smile. The Duchess lingers by the car door, precious effigy bundled against her chest. I let them in from the cold and lead them to their beds to sleep. In the morning, I leave them with food and go to work, thus far unaffected by the deity.

When I come home they are ensconced in my living room, religious offerings scattered about the floor. Plastic figures and lettered blocks, colourful picture books and plush animals that squeak when you tread on them. The tiny god crawls between his offerings, selecting a favoured item and displaying it to the faithful. They coo and praise his name, finding more figures to receive his blessings.

The tiny god considers me. I bring no offerings. I do not kneel and whisper his name in prayer. He throws back his head and wails in despair. I go to the kitchen to make dinner. Everyone else is too busy pandering to the needs of a teary idol.

It continues.

For weeks.

For months.

Visitors start to arrive.

They seem normal at first, and then the tiny god appears before them. Their eyes soften, their mouths forming wordless murmurings of adoration. They reach out in wonder and gather him into their arms. They sit for hours, stroking his hair and face, lost in rapture.

The flock grows, drawn by a mindless love. My home has become a temple in which I feel I no longer belong.

I carry on. Working, cooking, stepping over the ever-growing display of god-related artefacts. I constantly hoover the crumbs and clutter he leaves behind. The people who were once my friends do nothing but try to show me pictures or recite tales of the miraculous doings that occurred during the day.

I remain unmoved.

Settling into a comfortable seat one evening, I find myself under scrutiny. Blue eyes under a tousle of fine blonde hair consider me with great interest. I register his interest and turn to the TV. His watchfulness continues unabated, but I give no further heed until an awed gasp draws my attention. The Duke and Duchess both hold their breath, eyes fixated on the tiny god. He has crawled to the edge of my chair. He uses the furnishings to pull himself to standing, and on unsteady feet with arms held out in demand, he totters the two final steps to me.

I sigh, scoop him up before he can fall, and place him on my knee. He gurgles at me in contentment while the Duke and Duchess turn blue from breath-holding.

"Look," I explain. "It's not that I'm rejecting you, you seem nice. I just don't worship like everyone else."

He wriggles, and I set him back on the floor. He crawls to the Duke and Duchess who fawn in delighted psalms over his achievement. First steps are a big deal, apparently.

Tiny god seems content that I can be turned if necessary and never bothers me again.

31

The Duke and Duchess leave a few weeks after that. They take their tiny god with them.

A little later still, I find a photograph of him tucked between some of my belongings. They must have misplaced it when they moved. We've lost contact; I cannot return it.

I put it in the bin; it holds no meaning for me.

Even tiny gods can be wrong.

Eleven Days 'til Sunday

THE STRAPS of my duffel bag take turns falling off my shoulder and my backpack is relentless in its efforts to tip me. After several sweaty minutes, I make it to the hallway where once cream-colored paint has turned grey, save for the stains splattered and sprayed every which way.

Some of the doors have numbers. Some don't. 307 does, though the seven is drawn on with a marker. This is my room for the week and I force the key into the shaky lock, near a snap of rage when it swings open and an exceptionally bony girl covered in tattoos stands in front of me.

"Hey, I'm Kimmie."

"Oh, hey."

I get all of my miserable crap inside the room and ditch what I can on the bed Kimmie doesn't appear to be using.

"You work today?" I ask.

"Yeah, there's no one down there."

"You live here?"

"Nah, Campbell River. Me an' my ol' man got into a scrap and I had to get out the house. Didn't tell him where I was going. Let 'im tweak a little, you know?"

The room smells of her cheap body spray, the sulfur of matches burned in the bathroom and 80+ years of whatever else has gone wrong here.

"How long you been dancing?" she asks in a sandpapery voice.

"I started last week at The Lion's Den last week and now here."

"A rookie, eh? I'm surprised Randy sent you here."

"Why?"

She shrugs. "They usually send you to the nice places first. Make ya think it's all glamorous or somethin'."

"He needed a fill in. Said he'd owe me a favor."

"Yeah, Caramel Sunday didn't show up. Knowing her she g-holed or overdosed or some shit. Hey, where are you next week?"

"I'm here for two weeks. Well, eleven days now since it's already Wednesday."

"You doing the island tour?"

"Uh-huh. Campbell River next week."

She scoffs like I've said the wrong thing even though I am trying so hard not to.

"If you see my ol' man at JJ's tell him he's a fuckin' goof, alright?!"

I nod, a little frightened of the change in her mostly cordial tone.

"You know 'im? Dave? Beard? Rides a silver Panhead?"

"No, nuh-uh. Don't know any Daves."

She looks at me suspiciously, as though I might be the problem between her and bearded Dave.

"You have to cover your tattoos to work here?" I ask. We need to move on from Dave.

She laughs. "Nobody's lookin' at my arms and legs. They don't care none 'bout some ink."

"Can we open a window?"

"Good idea. I need a smoke."

She lights a cigarette and yanks upward on the window that looks out onto the snow covered roof-top. It doesn't budge and the room starts to fill with smoke. I try not to cough as I join the effort, pulling as hard as I can on the

34

two metal handles, but it's painted shut. It is the only spot in the entire building that has seen a fresh coat of paint since it was built. What luck.

"Do we have a schedule yet?"

"Yeah, it's on the mirror. It goes me, then you, then me, then you extretera, extretera."

The mirror has several lipstick prints on it and I wonder about the girls that have come before me and why they felt okay about putting their lips on such a revolting surface.

I'm on stage at noon tomorrow, then three, six and nine pm et cetera, et cetera.

I hang my costumes as best I can from the bent metal hangers in the closet and take a shower that leaves me feeling like I am becoming one with this room and like the only difference between Kimmie and I are tattoos and poor diction.

It's snowing again. Small, hard pellets hit my windshield as I drive into town and go through the Wendy's drive-thru. I sit in the parking lot wondering what my grandma would think if she knew I was so close by. Maybe I'll spend the day with her before I drive to the next shit hole. I'll lie to her about what I'm doing. I'll let her think I'm a receptionist at the gym working my way up to $14 an hour and free aerobics classes and she'll believe me because she can hardly remember my name.

When I get back to the room, Kimmie is smoking cocaine from a piece of tin foil. She swears each time she burns her thumb on the spark wheel of her yellow lighter. I'm grateful that she doesn't notice me come in as I lay down with all of my clothes on, careful not to let my skin touch anything. Through the thin walls, I can hear a loose, phlegmy cough.

I wake the next morning to Kimmie's guttural snore and think about the filthy state of a windpipe that emits such vile sounds.

There is no one in the bar when I arrive for my first show. A dozen or so tables are strewn about the room with folding metal chairs of various heights. One of them hosts a plate with some toast crusts and a few cold fries on it. Ants are spreading the word about it, however it is they do that, and I watch them scurry and scuttle, thrilled with their find. There's a neon Budweiser sign on the fritz and it flashes and pops, its tinny hum the only sound in the place.

I give my tape to the bartender and she looks me up and down in my red sequined dress, far too posh for an empty bar in a town of millworkers and fishermen and I feel apologetic for it even though the costumes are my favorite part of this whole endeavor. No where else in my life do I have the occasion to wear sequins, lace gloves, or hot pink PVC. With each elaborate get-up comes the accompaniment of my new alter-ego, Desiree Brooks. Desiree is confident, daring and nearly 6 inches taller in her stilettos. She thinks that stripping is the kind of career that might make her interesting and that all the men who desire her will make up for the one that left when she was a baby.

"We gotta wait 'til at least three people in the bar before I put choo on," crowed the frumpy barmaid.

"Sure."

"You take a seat here and I'll give you the wave when it's time."

I plunk down on the swivel stool with my blanket in my lap and look around. Posters of my predecessors hang on the wall, their autographed butts in the air and pumped-up tits showing through trashy school girl uniforms and faux nurse's attire. When I got my tonsils out I don't remember any nurses in white satin mini-dresses or tiny paper hats adorned with red crosses, but a stripper's interpretation of reality varies a lot from a civilian's.

A man with a thin combover and no front teeth shuffles up to the bar in house slippers. Without saying anything the barmaid slides a coffee across the counter and plunks three sugar cubes in it and a shot of whiskey beside, while he fumbles for some change.

He turns his unshaven face to me. "You the stripper?"

I nod, feeling exposed by the rhetorical question.

"I'm Arvin." He shuffles into the darkness until I can barely make out his gargoyle-like silhouette at a corner table.

Twenty minutes later a group of three come. Two of them sidle up to front row while the third goes to the bar and gets a pitcher of beer. He looks me over and I try to be Desiree.

"Hi." I squeak baring my teeth in what I mean to be a smile.

He tips his greasy baseball hat and nods, "Hey, darlin'."

I hear my song come on and the bartender wags her finger in my direction.

I strut across the stage, begging my ankles not to give way as I make my way to the pole.

Desiree takes over. She wiggles and jiggles, twists and spreads and listens to the music instead of the lewd commentary from the men just inches from her naked vagina.

The one with the goatee is especially attentive. She can't see his eyes, but she knows they're on her and she likes that he's interested, even if it is for the wrong reasons.

She slides her naked back down the pole, kicking one leg way up and steadying herself with the other. She is still working on this move and hits the floor with her tailbone harder than she would like. She grimaces through the pain and Arvin winces when he hears the thud from his seat in the corner though she can't see him.

Goatee puts a five-dollar bill on the stage and she personalizes the show for him, bending over and spreading her labia with her manicured nails. The nails still feel awkward. She can't do up her jeans or pick up change if a cashier puts it on the counter, but they are part of the image she now adheres to.

Her last song stops abruptly and she hopes that the ghetto blaster hasn't chewed up her tape as she picks up her fuzzy blanket and wraps it around her nakedness, tucking it securely under her armpits. She bends to pick up her tip and Goatee speaks.

"You wanna come join us for a drink, hon?"

She doesn't have a response ready for this yet.

"Oh, um, sure."

Upstairs Kimmie is frantically throwing costumes around apparently looking for something. "You seen my Mötley Crüe set?" she barks accusingly.

"Your music?"

She stares at me long enough to be uncomfortable. "Nevermind, I think I left it in my truck. Who's down there?"

"I dunno, like three guys in the front and some guy named Arvin."

"He was in a bad accident and everyone died, Irene said."

"Who's Irene?"

"Oh, fuck yeah! Here's my tape! Right on, man I always dance to Crüe first set."

She slams the door behind her and I hear her clomp down the stairs like a Clydesdale. There's over an hour 'til her show, but maybe she can't tell time.

I'm not sure what to wear back down to the bar. Are those guys expecting Desiree? I have to get these shoes off my feet, so I put on my real clothes and my real shoes and feel real weird when I greet Goatee and his friends with excruciatingly dirty fingernails. They are machinists and I don't care what that means, but I know I never want a finger that dirty inside of me.

We sit and drink. I have three vodka cranberries and a shot of Jameson. We seem to be in celebratory mode now, maybe because we're getting along so well and they're so

38

attentive. Roy, the only name I can remember because I have an uncle called that, is giving me a foot rub and I almost fall asleep because it feels so good and my feet are so tired of being crammed into those silly heels. Small town guys are really nice.

I'm jolted awake when Kimmie comes on stage singing loudly to her rock music and yelling with a force usually reserved for someone trying to save her child from being hit by a bus.

"Clap you motherfuckers! You wanna see these titties or what?!"

No wonder her wind pipe is so thrashed.

My new friends clap and whistle and Goatee stands up and lifts his shirt, dancing like a buffoon. Halfway through her first song it's like I no longer exist to them. Roy has abandoned the massage and I put my shoes back on and sit up as straight as I can. I stand, hoping one of them will notice, but I slip out the fire exit without a nod.

The air smacks me boldly from my sloppiness and I feel tears in my eyes. It's hard to decipher what they are for.

There's a pay phone across the parking lot and I think about calling someone, but who? I walk over anyway, wanting a purpose. I step inside the booth and lean against the glass, pushing my head against its cold. I pick up the receiver and push the buttons listening to the beeps and boops they make in my ear. The reality makes me ache.

Across the lot I see Roy and Goatee come out and light cigarettes. I turn my back to them and the phone utters a cacophony of warnings for me to hang up if I'm not actually serious about making a call. I put down the receiver and see Roy making his way over as Goatee's back is swallowed by the door and he returns to the bar.

Roy and I sit on the curb and smoke. I just hold mine because it makes me sick. I can smell his breath and I'm aware that he's too close to me, but it's okay until it suddenly isn't.

I stand up. "I've got a show soon. I should go get ready."

"Nah, there's no one in there."

"Really? I hope they don't cancel it. I don't get paid if it's canceled."

"I'll pay ya to sit out here with me."

"I'm freezing."

"Yeah, it's cold as a witch's tit. I'll go warm up my truck and we can hang out in there."

I'm sobering up. "I'm just gonna go inside, maybe get something to eat. I haven't eaten anything yet today."

He pulls a chocolate bar out of his flannel pocket.

"You like Mars bars?"

I eat it in 3 or 4 very grateful bites, feeling a peanut fall in my lap, but chewing too voraciously to stop and pick it up.

Roy laughs, revealing a gold-outlined eye tooth. "You need someone to take care of you, don't you?"

"I should get back." I stand to walk, less wobbly now, energized by the sugar.

I'm almost to the door when he grabs my wrist. "Hey, don't go yet." His nose is red and its blackheads make him the ugliest man in the world.

"I'll see you later. Thanks for the chocolate."

"Oh, so it's like that, eh? Let me buy ya drinks, smoke my smokes, eat my food, lead me on and then take off?"

"I don't even smoke."

I am about 3 feet from the door when I see it rock a little and then open slowly as if the person on the other side has the strength of a newly born fawn. Arvin, the guy that drinks whiskey with his coffee, hunches over, trying to light his pipe.

"Marvin!" I shouted far too loudly.

He nods, politely, without correcting me.

"You gonna go use him now then?" Roy hisses.

I walk toward Arvin and fall into him when I trip over the curb. He catches me and we sway like saplings in a

40

windstorm. I hold onto his neck, feeling its warmth and the softness of the downy hair that still clings to his head. His arms are around my waist I think, and we steady each other after 20 precarious seconds in which we might both tumble to the ground. At first all I can hear is Roy's steel-toed boots staggering away, as he mutters words like bitch and freeloader, but when he is gone, there are breathy sobs, teeth chattering and noses sucking back snot and whose sounds are whose doesn't matter. Arvin and I stand in each other's arms crying hard for a good long while before I untangle myself and hear him say softly, "Sorry."

I climb the stairs two at a time wanting to get away quickly and quietly like a jaguar. I wipe dripping mascara from my face and watch my spray tan streak across the back of my hand.

Kimmie is smoking from her tin foil again.

"Did nobody tell ya it's bad fuckin' manners to sit in gyno when another broad's on stage?"

"What?"

"Don't be such an attention whore. You get your eighteen minutes on stage."

"Sorry."

"Have you been crying?"

"No, I'm good."

"It's alright. I'm just trying to look out for you. Some chicks get pissed about that shit."

By Friday I know that I have to be Desiree in all my interactions. With Kimmie, with the men in the bar, with the bartenders that try to get me to wait for them to finish their phone calls before they put me on stage.

"Hey, it's 2:05," I bark, pointing at my watch letting them know that I am the fucking priority.

After listening to her call him a limp dick cocksucker and a piece of shit loser, for three days Kimmie decides to

41

leave early and go back to Dave.

"I'm sure he's pretty horny by now, he'll treat me right for a few days."

"You'd leave me here?"

She looks right through me like she's never seen me before.

Dave comes to pick her up after her first show and I am left alone in the room.

By Monday the rancidity seeping in from the hallway makes me miss the smell of her body spray and charbroiled drugs.

I'm the only dancer here now and while the agents try to find a replacement I have to do shows every hour and a half instead of every three. There isn't much turnover in the crowd and they are as sick of me as I am of them. I have to repeat costumes and my back aches from arching it. Thank God, I haven't seen Arvin or Roy again though. I wouldn't know how to act.

After the voices underneath my window quiet down that night and the floor stops shaking from the music, a silence seeps into my bones and hangs out there like a pack of teenagers loitering in a food court. I miss everyone I can think of and people I've never met.

The bed creaks under my weight as I let out a breath I hadn't realized I was holding. I think about smashing a pane of the window to get some air in here, but I worry I will freeze solid and someone will have to tell my grandma what I am doing in a place like this.

Sunday I only have four shows since even the degenerates that hang out in strip clubs all day have families to be with. I'm too tired to do much and I wish I could just watch TV, but this place is getting to me, so I go to the Tim Horton's between shows and play solitaire and drink black coffee because it seems edgier than cream and sugar.

When I get back, the hallway still smells like rotting garbage and the contrast of the coffee and donut break I've just given my nose makes it less tolerable. I burn the incense I tucked in the front pocket of my suitcase and tuck a dirty towel under the door to fill the gap.

When I come down for my last show on Friday night Irene is talking to the cook. I hear Arvin's name, but I can't tell what they're saying with the hockey game playing loudly on the radio. Maybe they know why he was crying last week. Maybe that's why he hasn't been back.

I mention the stink upstairs, but she doesn't care.

I finish yet another strip show mirroring the lack of enthusiasm from the men that have seen my naked body nearly as many times as their spouse's by now. I jog up the stairs to get into my room as fast as I can and twist my ankle hearing myself screech in pain. The gasp of air I involuntarily suck in is so foul I gag as I hobble to 307.

I fall asleep at some point and awaken to heavy footsteps, walkie talkies and the snapping of a stretcher being assembled. I get dressed and stick my head into the hallway to see a black bag being wheeled by and a man with a jacket that says Coroner on the back.

I cover my mouth, feeling the contents of my stomach push between my fingers.

"You should go back inside ma'am," a clean-cut young fireman says professionally.

A lady in a uniform hands me a handful of tissues and a kidney bean shaped tray to throw up in. The rest of the crew move through the hallway and we are alone.

"I'm sorry about your neighbor," she says gently.

"I don't live here."

"Did you know him?"

"I don't know anyone."

She looks at me curiously.

"I mean I don't know anyone here. I'm just, I'm just here 'til Sunday."

43

"He's lived here a long time, but he liked his privacy apparently. Hotel will be shut down for contamination, I reckon. You have somewhere else to go?"

"Who was he?"

She looks inside her metal clipboard. "Arvin Livingston."

I fall back against the door, feeling the paint chips on the backs of my arms.

Arvin.

"I did know him. He had a cough."

"I'm sorry."

She puts a warm hand on my forearm and I see eyes that feel sorry for me. I pull away, close the door and pack my things to move to the next town.

Mr. Bitterbeans

THE BARISTAS were all too goddamn small, thought Hunt as he inched his way up the queue. It wasn't a problem with the girls, pretty pixies one and all, although the sight of their tiny hands sent an uncomfortable shiver through him all the same – a shiver that would echo back as he reached out his comparatively big paws to receive his latte and his change. It was the male ones that really bothered him; you just couldn't trust a short man.

Their inadequate frames were rammed to the gills with all manner of nastiness, so eager were they to exact revenge on people of normal stature, Hunt had always found. He made sure he kept a sticky eyeball on them whenever they prepared his coffee for they were sure to spit in it given half the chance, and their saliva could cause you to shrink. Why would anyone, Hunt wondered for the umpteenth time, hire such repulsive imps to serve a decent paying member of the public?

He couldn't help but breathe a sigh of relief when one of the girls took his order; not one of the Lolita dolls but a plump little thing, plain as brown bread with a toothy smile he could not bring himself to return...they reminded him too much of...

When he prised the lid off his latte to sprinkle in his usual three sachets of sugar his heart skipped and skidded; the leafy pattern on top of the milk, the one he so admired and which made the coffee somehow taste expensive, wasn't there.

It had been replaced by a large frothy loveheart.

Yes, that was definitely what it was, there could be no mistake; Hunt stared at with a rapturous intensity until an impatient cough behind him moved him along. He risked a quick glance over to the barista but she was busy and he could not catch her eye. He hung around the sugar station to surreptitiously check out the coffee of others to see if it were the same – it might just be a promotional thing, or even just a quirk she had – but no, only his beverage bore the gloopy badge of love; it was a message, a declaration, a statement of intent intended for his eyes only.

He went back daily, timing it so that she always served him.

He practised smiling. Sometimes she would flip him a wink as she handed over his drink, her fingers touching his for a brief lingering eternity. Although Hunt loved a smoke with his daily caffeine hit he began to have his latte inside so that he could watch his goddess barista as he sipped at it slowly. This could have been a disastrous mistake; with no lid to cover her secret greeting, would she be bold enough to leave her mark for all to see?

His fears were allayed by the very first cup; the heart floated shamelessly there as his own soared at the sight of it. He felt himself a king, fuelled by life's two greatest gifts – love and coffee. They wrote songs about love, poetry too, but coffee was important too; why else would they chop down a rainforest just so that he could stir it?

'See that?' Hunt said, pointing out the heart to some guy seated opposite. He was the kind of person Hunt would never normally speak to, the kind with big headphones and man-bun hair, the kind with a laptop and fussy cupcake.

'See what?' asked the man, leaning over; he was wearing a suit jacket over a t-shirt that; oh, how outrageous you are, Hunt sneered inwardly, how bohemian.

'It's a heart of course...a loveheart! That really cute

46

barista over there always adorns my morning java with a token of her affection.'

The geek adjusted his headphones and went back to tapping out nonsense on his laptop; 'Looks more like a clot to me.'

You're the fucking clot, Hunt wanted to yell in his face, a fucking boil, then throw his coffee into his trimmed pencil line beard and scald the smug ignorance off his thin lips. He smiled sweetly instead; sweet as the heart that rocked gently on an archipelago of four brown sugars.

'You're not even a man, you techno obsessed freak,' Hunt said quietly; 'What would you know of love when you're half machine?' The man tapped on, nodding his head to the beat of his headphones, oblivious of Hunt's contempt. He wondered if he should take off his shirt and show the geek the modifications he had made to his own splendid body – but what if the barista saw his improvements and winced? She might not be ready, she might not understand.

The hearts grew smaller as the days pressed on and Hunt procrastinated about how to ask his beloved barista out; the smiles dwindled too, right down to a thin terse line that made him shiver. She thinks I'm weird, he reasoned, because I stare. The only way to prove her wrong was simple; he had to make her jealous. Women were irrational, fuelled by jealousy, everyone knew that.

Hunt felt certain if he were to conduct some kind of showy liaison in front of her, thus proving he was attractive and normal, it would instil a competitive instinct in her that would see her fight tooth and nail to claim him. It would bring her to her senses and the milky hearts would soon return.

He scanned the coffee shop for a likely, and disposable, candidate and found one almost immediately; the world was, after all, full of throwaway girls. She wore a bobble hat to show she was 'kooky', her overloud conversation hitting

47

all the 'right on' bullet points; Uni, adventures of the gap
year, volunteer work and its importance to 'y'know, like,
my personal growth'.

He opened his mouth unsure if he were about to yawn or
vomit; he tried to tune her out, select someone else, but her
prattling took an unexpected turn that reeled him back in
again.

'One time in Amsterdam,' she was telling her coterie of
bland friends, 'I went to this, like, fuck club, you know? It
really opened my eyes. We are so uptight over our sexuality
here, I'm not even kidding. Seriously, I enjoyed it so much
– it gave me licence to explore what turns me on as, you
know, a sexual being.'

Her dippy little mates giggled at her brazenness but she
swatted them aside with a superiority born of self
adoration and began pontificating on anal beads,
threesomes, and the judicious use of drugs to prolong the
climax. Hunt knew that as soon as she left her rapt
audience would scorn her for the slut she so obviously was,
but he didn't hang around long enough to eavesdrop on
their backstabbing.

Now was his chance. He waited until she was passing his
beloved barista by the counter before pouncing, grabbing
the bobble-hatted whore by her tits and shouting that he
loved her; he was such a good actor for in truth he felt
nothing for her at all. She screamed all colours of murder,
breaking down in snot nosed fear – the bitch was a total
fraud, an unbelievable hypocrite. Hunt had no time for her
hysterics, or the approach of several burly customers intent
on making hero headlines, he only had eyes for his pretty
little barista.

She looked even more frightened than the bobble-hatted
liar; her face was all scrunched up, her hand trembling as
she pointed at him, mouthing something to her manager
about a 'psycho'. Hunt had been called that before and it
always had the same effect – it always removed the scales

from his eyes and showed him the world for what it really was.

How could I have been so stupid? Hunt cursed, jumping the pot plants and racing from the coffee shop. Now that he had gotten a good look at his barista he saw she was overweight, vindictive, and sweaty. She wasn't fit for his jars. Hunt didn't like to think of his jars but the fat bitch had forced him to. How could I have been so stupid, again?

He fled to his car. The mall was no longer safe for him; the coffee tramp and the blubbery barista had made damn sure of that. Still, he mused, as he drove aimlessly around waiting for his tears to dry, that had been the best romance in so long; at least he hadn't proposed this time.

It was time to stop kidding himself where women were concerned, time to wake up and smell the...

No, Hunt was finished with that foul drink – the very word stank of her betrayal. Of all their betrayals. He was a tea man from here on in; tea was plain but it was honest. Tea went with everything. Hunt made a list of all the things tea went with until his belly rumbled. He skidded to a halt outside the first cafe he came across.

The carpark of The Brown Dot was filled with trucks and its windows with dying wasps; no Fancy Dan branding here, no geek boys with gadgets and ridiculous footwear, just plain working man's fayre. Hunt pulled open the paint chipped door, breathing in an oily tsunami, shaking loose a storm of dust from the once white net curtains. He stood awhile, allowing his eyes time to adjust to the dim fug; yes, he thought, this is where I belong, these are my people.

'I haven't seen you in here before,' said a smudge by the till; the counter was as shiny and as treacherous as a skating rink. Hunt walked toward the voice until the blurred figure revealed itself to be an obese female who seemed to be perspiring pure lard. 'You lost or something?'

'No, I'm...,' began Hunt defensively, gauging the distance to the door.

'I'm only ribbing you,' said the porker, her voice lighting up the dingy cafe. 'I'm Sally; Sally the Server, that's what they call me. What do they call you then?'

Hunt thought of the judgemental barista, of all the ones before her, and of the jar in his fridge that seemed to stare back at him in contempt; they call me lovelorn, fool, pariah dog. He swallowed drily, tasting foul coffee in his throat, tasting her undigested memory, a memory that was a pile of –

'Bitterbeans.'

'Excuse me?' Sally raised a well plucked brow.

'My name is Mr. Bitterbeans.'

She gave a little chuckle, her eyes sparkling like mica chips through the grease; 'And what can I get for you, Mr Bitterbeans?'

'I'll have tea, not coffee. Tea. And a burger, toasted bap, no onions, no salad, just plain with a hefty dollop of relish. And tea.'

'Oh, I like a man who's particular. Sit down, pet, take a pew, and I'll bring it over to you in two ticks.'

Her smile had him buzzing; she wasn't fat at all, she was really rather pretty when you looked at her properly. He took a seat by a large, stubbly, balloon of a man who was attempting to read a tabloid through a thick nest of facial hair; his hands were so covered in oil it looked as if he might be secreting the stuff.

Hunt sniffed the air, catching the scent of Sally's perfume – an angel fart in an abattoir – just behind him. Proffering him a chipped cup, she plonked down his burger on the graffiti strewn table; 'Tea's on the house, dear,' she said, 'newcomers always drink for free the first time, at least they do on my shift.'

Hunt waited until she was gone before flipping the bun off his burger to make sure it had been made to his exact specifications; he caught his breath as a familiar warm glow enveloped him.

50

'Look at that,' he said to the truck driver opposite – well, what else could he be? A man that rotund could not fit into a regular sized vehicle. Hunt pushed the burger under the trucker's nose, pointing at the heart shaped dab of relish in its greasy centre.

'Look at what?' the big man asked, nonplussed, over the top of his paper.

'It's a loveheart.'

The trucker shrugged; 'Looks more like Sally cleared her throat on it to me.'

Hunt didn't know why he had even bothered speaking to him in the first place; he was more engine than man – probably had a battery instead of a heart. Hunt retrieved his burger quickly in case the fat philistine gobbled it up.

He sneaked a peek over toward the till; Sally beamed and gave him a dainty little finger wave that left smears on the air. Everyone was so big here – they were big because, unlike scrawny little coffee girls, they were full to the seams with love. Yet, waving shyly back at Sally, he was struck by the desire to return to see his barista; although brief, their love had been special and it seemed only natural to keep a memento of it.

There was the rub – where would he keep a memento, when he had so many already?

The deep freeze was full of nipples and other sundries. His fridge was as good a place as any, but it too was becoming crammed. Maybe if he cleared out some of his jars of eyes (he had too many eyes) but he could not bring himself to part with any of them, even the ones that resembled hailstones; for those were the children's eyes, and a child's love was the most precious of all.

Still, he would have to be ruthless and have a clear-out. He looked down at the red relish heart and sighed; there was every indication that this burgeoning romance with Sally was, finally, going to be the real thing.

ROBERT DOMINICK

Home Team

IT STARTS when you're young. Your dad buys you a mini jersey, a mini hat, maybe a pair of mini shorts. You're only a year old, so you don't remember any of this, of course, unless it's preserved in photographic form.

But it happens.

Driving down to the stadium, your dad tells you all he knows about this glorious game they call football:

"Now, those big uglies up front are called the offensive lineman, and their job is to protect the guy who throws the ball. He's the quarterback, and the guy behind him is called the running back. I'm not going to explain what he does, 'cause it's kind of self-explanatory, don't you think?"

You're only one year old, so you don't really understand. He wants a nod of understanding, but you can only provide him with your one-two punch, a spot of drool on your chin and a soft sigh. He pats you on the head, anyway.

As the years go on, you become an ardent fan. At five, you go to your first playoff game. At eight, your dad enters you in the ten-year-old division of the Run, Punt, Pass, and Kick competition. You easily beat some kid named Keith

Malone, but you don't gloat. It's not part of the game.

In high school, you play linebacker on the football team and dominate every defense you face. The leaves change, and winters come, but your passion for football remains consistent. Going down to the stadium on Sundays for every home game becomes a weekly ritual (your dad put in for season tickets the day you were born). The painted faces and loud voices that frightened you when you first went to the stadium no longer do so; you are now one of these faces, one of these voices.

Sometimes your dad will buy you a beer at the game. You don't know what to say, so you just sip it quietly, putting it down only when the home team does something truly worthy. It tastes bitter, yet sweet at the same time. Maybe it's nothing in the beer; maybe it's the atmosphere. You ponder this for a moment, but only for a moment, and you go on drinking your beer.

Sometimes you have to drive home from the stadium because your dad can't.

On Mondays, you sit in your classes and discuss the game the day before. You talk about the hardest hits, the game-winning plays, the stout defense, everything. Keith Malone is now one of your best friends. You play together on the football team, date similar-looking girls, and prefer the same type of beer. Years later, Keith will be the best man at your wedding.

For college, you leave your home, but you do not abandon your team. It's always there in the front of your mind. You make fun of the football team that everyone cheers for at your college. You decorate your room with posters, have a picture of your favorite player as the background on your laptop, and find other fans just like you who root for the same team. When your team comes to play in the city where you go to school, you of course get tickets. On Sunday, you get to the stadium early, proudly wearing your team colors. You tailgate, get so drunk you throw up in the parking lot, sober up, and yell at the top of your lungs during the game with bloodshot eyes and a pounding headache. It doesn't matter; it's your team.

Someone yells, "Shut up, asshole!" when the home team is down and you're too loud. It doesn't matter. Your team wins anyway.

You make a home in this new city, but never forget where home really is, halfway across the state.

When you come home for breaks, you and your dad watch football on Sundays just like always. You have a beer; you've gotten used to the taste by now. You hug him, kiss your mother on the cheek, and embark on the five-hour journey that waits ahead of you.

Years pass, and things change, but not your team. You've gotten used to the heartbreak, the missed opportunities, the playoff meltdowns. Your parents die.

You renew your dad's season tickets: he would've wanted it that way.

You get married. When your future wife says, "I do," she has no idea what she is getting into, but she doesn't care. The next year, you have a son. His eyes are blue, like your dad's. You can't believe you created something so beautiful. You cry, the first time since your dad's funeral.

You go to Dick's the next day. Keith works as the manager. He offers you congratulations on the new baby. You hug him, tell him "Thanks," and walk towards the mini jerseys.

Across The Golden Gate

DURING THE FIRST THREE MONTHS of my freshman year of college three things left me wanting to come home for a break by Thanksgiving; my roommate's boyfriend who was always in our room and smelled of beer and sweat, my chemistry lab with its ten hours of weekly homework, and the weird tuna dish that was a Friday staple on the cafeteria's dinner menu. I missed my own bedroom with its pink drapes, and a closet full of Midwestern winter clothes I didn't need with me in San Diego. My parents had other ideas, however, and they traveled to my aunt's house in Green Bay for Thanksgiving weekend, foisting me off on my older sister, Kate, who'd moved to San Francisco in spring.

"You two girls will have a great time together," my mother explained on the phone when I protested. "It's been so long since you've seen each other and I'm sure you'll have a lot to catch up on while you're there. You've always wanted to go to San Francisco ever since you wrote that report about it in sixth grade."

"I also wanted to be a ballet dancer in sixth grade but I don't see you encouraging me to do that," I said.

"Of course not, dear. Your feet are too big," she said.

"Who is going to cook the turkey? Who will make the stuffing? I can't cook and lord knows Kate can't either."

The kitchen mishaps of my sister and I were family legend, from burnt rice crispy treats to roasted chicken so undercooked it nearly walked off the table.

"I'll send you the recipes and you two will figure it out."

My parents were enjoying their empty nest years and in their newfound freedom they clearly forgot Kate and I don't get along, never have gotten along and likely never would. Hopefully, we could get through Thanksgiving Day, I could wander San Francisco on my own for a day, then spend the last two days studying for my finals. As I packed the last few things the morning I left, I called Kate to remind her I was coming.

"Don't forget to pick me up at one-thirty."

"That's today, Missy? Already?"

"Yes. And it's Melissa." Kate was the only one who still called me by my baby name, a name I detested that had followed me from birth until I ditched it this year college. No matter how many times I told people to call me by my full name, they always returned to the nickname I'd abhorred since being called Prissy Sissy Missy by Bradley Goldstein in third grade.

"While you're here we can walk across the Golden Gate Bridge."

"Why would we do that? You're afraid of heights and I don't like anything remotely related to exercise."

"Everyone out here says you have to do it at least once," she said. "And you said you wanted to do it, you know, in that report you wrote on San Francisco."

"Why does everyone remember this report?" I said. " I have a lot of studying to do for my finals, so we won't have time."

"Finals, schminals!" Kate said. "I'll see you at two-thirty."

"One-thirty," I yelled but she'd already hung up.

I often dreamed of the maid of honor speech I'd give at Kate's wedding if she were to ask me. I'd start with stories about how she just went after what she wanted, like when my dad told her she couldn't be on the track team and have a job at the same time if it interfered with her grades, so she got straight A's, broke the school record for the 400-meter run and still worked two nights a week as a cashier at a party goods store. Then I'd say when she was put in charge, she took charge and I'd bring up the nights our parents went out leaving us home alone. Long parts of those nights consisted of Kate sitting on me, crushing my ribs while I screamed that I couldn't breathe. I'd then say if she wanted to go out with a boy, she didn't wait for him to ask her, she went right up to him and told him when to pick her up and where she wanted to go. I'd say how she was the lead in all the school plays and when she came home from rehearsal, she'd stay in character, eating dinner as the lovelorn Kim McAfee from Bye, Bye Birdie. I'd close by saying I wished I was more like her and I'm glad we'd gotten close as adults. But that last part wasn't true at all. I was happy keeping to myself and we were not close. I never reached for the heights that Kate did. I was never the best at anything, never the lead in the play and I was okay with that. I was happy to toil away doing what I was doing and staying out of the spotlight. Kate had exhausted my parents with her ever-hectic schedule. I was almost free to go as I pleased as long as I came home on time and my grades were good.

But there I was, waiting at the airport in San Francisco on the busiest travel day of the year and Kate was late and not answering her cell phone. After I left a third message on her voice mail, I plopped down on a bench near the baggage carousel and pulled out my Psychology textbook. My Psych final was next week and I was having a hard time staying awake in class. It was my only eight a.m. class and the professor's soft nasally voice droned on as the perfect sleep aid no amount of sugar spiked coffee could overcome. After twenty minutes of waiting and four pages of incomprehensible psych babble Kate finally appeared.

"Boo, Missy," she said.

"You're late," I said. "And it's Melissa."

Kate stood there with a half-smile on her face. She made no movement towards me for a hug or even a handshake, my sister who I hadn't seen since my high school graduation in June. She was wearing pink sweatpants and a white t-shirt and her hair was hastily pulled back, stray strands splayed across her face.

"Sorry about that," she said. "I'm having trouble keeping track of time these days."

She gave me the once over, running her eyes up and down looking for something disapproving to say. She took her time. I'm sure she found several things but chose the most hurtful before saying it with just the right nuance to sound like a compliment.

"It's good to see you're keeping your skin protected from the Southern California sun," she said. "Your arms are as pale as ever."

Mission accomplished.

"I didn't go there to get a tan," I said. "I'm there for school." She turned her eyes back to her phone which she clutched in her left hand.

"I'm just saying it wouldn't hurt to sit outside occasionally while studying. You could have stayed inside all winter in Madison"

Kate picked up the lightest of my three bags and left me with the backpack loaded with books and the giant suitcase with the wobbly wheel.

"You sure brought a lot of stuff for two days," she said.

"What do you mean two days?" I asked. "I don't fly back until Monday morning."

"Mom told me you were going back on Friday. Great. The whole weekend is completely shot. What if I had plans for the rest of the weekend? I don't just sit around waiting for family to visit."

"Hey, don't be mad at me, I didn't arrange this trip. I could be with my roommate's family in Carlsbad hanging out in a beachfront mansion. Be mad at Mom. This was her idea."

"She told me you wanted to come up here," Kate said.

My anger with my mother was brewing over now.

"Clearly Mom had some plan for us that she didn't want to share. I guess we are supposed to figure it out on our own."

"Let's go walk the bridge, take a picture and send it to Mom and Dad and get on with it. We can stop by my place first. It's on the way to the bridge anyway."

We stuffed my bags into the trunk of Kate's Ford Escort among the mess of blankets, shoes, and a case of water bottles. Kate talked about how great it was to be in San Francisco, about the restaurant Reginald had taken her where she had the best tomato salad she'd ever had. I listened just well enough to hear the important words so I could ask her another leading question so she could continue her story which I then tuned out.

"What kind of tomatoes?" I asked.

She read of a list of them: heirloom, plum, green plum, Brazilian cherry, something called baby red. I never knew there were this many kinds of tomatoes nor did I care. I pulled my Psychology book out from my bag.

"What is Reginald doing this weekend?" I asked.

"Family stuff, I guess," Kate said. "I don't think his parents like me."

I opened the book to the chapter on psychoanalysis, heavy on the Freud, and tried again to comprehend the words.

"Am I boring you?" Kate asked.

"No, I just have a big test when I get back Monday and I'm way behind." I wasn't bored but if we were going to make it through the weekend without running out of things to talk about, we needed to pace ourselves.

Kate pulled her phone out, dialed a number on her phone and started talking to someone named Rachel, carrying on as if I were not even in the car. She ended the call with "Call me tomorrow night and we'll go out," as she pulled into a parking spot in front of her apartment.

"Here we are," Kate said.

Her building looked old, really old. Older than 1906 when the great earthquake and fire wiped out most of San Francisco. It had illegible graffiti on the exterior door and what looked like smoke stains across the brick. Junk mail piled up on the floor of the lobby. The inside door was heavy and creaked as it opened. The carpet in the hallway smelled heavily of must.

"Nice place," I said, but Kate read my sarcasm. "Is this the worst neighborhood in San Fran?"

"I know it's a dump but it's all I could afford," she said. "I don't want to live in Oakland. And for the record, no one who lives here calls it San Fran. We call it San Francisco."

We carried the bags up the three flights of stairs. She pointed me to the couch where I'd be sleeping; an old brown sagging couch that looked like it was the Ikea floor model, sat on by thousands of random shoppers before being picked out of the discount section. I changed clothes and then we headed back down to her car to tackle the bridge.

* * *

When we got out of the car and Kate looked up at the gleaming golden bridge connecting San Francisco to Marin County she was surprised how far up we had to go to even get to the bridge.

"Way up there?" she said. "All this time I've been here and it always looked closer."

"Don't look at me, this is your idea."

"Mom told me you wanted to do it."

"She was wrong. Were you even listening to what she was saying?"

"Not really. She always calls at bad times and drones on and on about where the cats are sleeping and what Dad is planting in the yard. It's hard to listen for very long."

The late afternoon sun was beginning its descent into the Pacific. We walked slowly at first, still quite a distance from the bridge. The gravel path wound up towards the bridge through a wooded park. Every step was uphill. I wasn't planning on doing much but eating and studying this weekend, so I wore jeans that were too loose and my beat-up sandals that provided little comfort or support. It was cooler here than San Diego so I had a long sleeve shirt on and had tied my San Diego State sweatshirt around my waist. Kate had switched to gym shoes and she perched her sunglasses atop her head. She had her cell phone in her hand as we walked like at any moment she could get a call that would rescue her from this tortuous task.

"How's work?" I asked.

"You know, it's a job. I'm not sure being a marketing assistant is what I want to do forever," she said.

"Wasn't there a chance you'd get to do graphic design, too?"

"That's what they said when they hired me but I don't think it is going to happen. They have less work now than when I started and they already let some people go. You know, the economy." Her voice wavered, some uncertainty that I'd never heard from her before. She'd always seemed so confident and sure.

The dirt path ended and we joined up with the sidewalk that ran along the side of US 101. The silence of the park gave way to the rushing noise of the traffic. For the first time, the bridge came into full view. The gentle horizontal curve of the bridge appeared to go on forever and the twin peaks of the bridge soared into the sky. The famous bay fog was nowhere to be seen. The sidewalk was more crowded than the path had been, people walked in both directions and cyclists weaved in and out of the walkers. We did our best to stay out of the way since everyone was moving faster than us. At times, it felt like we weren't even walking together or that we were even sisters but more like two strangers who just happened to be on the bridge at the same time walking the same pace, awkwardly aware of each other while trying not to show it. Occasionally, I'd look over just to make sure Kate was still next to me.

I knew there would come a point on this trip where we'd run out of things to talk about but I expected it'd take longer. We didn't talk a lot growing up, even when we shared a bedroom, so it shouldn't have surprised me. With others Kate would have no problem filling the time talking about herself but with me she didn't even make that effort. I couldn't take the silence anymore.

"This bridge is amazing," I said.

"Yeah, I guess," Kate answered. "You know, for a bridge."

"I read they have like thirty-five painters continuously painting the bridge, wherever it needs touch-ups?"

"Wow, useless facts about a big bridge. Thank you, Missy!"

We reached the point on the bridge where the giant bundle of orange cables began its rise from its concrete base to the top of the seven hundred fifty-foot towers. The sidewalk narrowed as it edged around the tower's footprint before widening again. The traffic whizzed past us just a few feet away. At first, I was on the right side overlooking the Bay and Kate was next to traffic but she stepped ahead of me to switch spots.

"The traffic is freaking me out a little," she said. "and there is no way I am going to look down."

The wind picked up and with heavy rush hour traffic we could feel the bridge sway. I felt a chill tingle across my skin, a mixture of the cool winds and a little fear. I peered over the edge down to the water below and saw what I thought were seagulls flying low over the small ripples breaking on the water's surface.

"How's Reginald," I asked.

"Don't ask," she said.

"Did something happen?"

"Don't ask means don't ask, not ask again."

She folded her arms across her waist and looked away. She walked faster. I tried to keep up but with my sandals I could barely stay with her. I'd clearly pressed a button.

We were at the mid-point of the bridge. We weren't talking. For a while I counted the vertical cables that came up from the deck of the bridge to the giant coil of cables but I quickly got bored of it. Then I noticed the blue signs on the light posts that said "Discuss Counseling. There is hope. Make the call," in bold letters with a phone number listed at the bottom. Did the signs represent the last chance to save the hopeless? It seemed comical to me that such a sign would make anyone who had come this far to the midpoint of the bridge reconsider jumping.

"Halfway done," Kate said.

"Well, half way across. We're only a quarter-way done. Once we get across all the way we are halfway done."

"Okay, Miss glass half empty," she said. "Let's take the picture and show Mom and Dad how much fun we're having."

At the midpoint of the bridge the giant suspension coil met the sidewalk. I pulled my camera from my pocket and asked a man who was walking the other way to take a picture of us. He looked at me for a second like he didn't understand what I was saying but eventually took the camera and stood waiting for us to get close together. Kate leaned into me. The camera flashed and the man handed it back to me without a word. Kate walked on as I looked at the picture: I had a big fake smile on my face but Kate couldn't even do that. She looked worried.

"Is something wrong, Kate?" I asked.

She stopped.

"Everything is wrong," she said. "Everything. Reginald broke up with me. In June. He met some girl at work he insists is his soulmate. He didn't even do it face to face. He sent me a text message and wouldn't call me back."

Guys don't break up with Kate. She tells them when their relationship is over.

"I'm sorry, sis."

"I moved here for him. I took a shitty job that I hate so I could be here with him, a shitty job I no longer have because I got fired."

"What?"

"It doesn't matter, I hated the job. I was lucky it lasted this long. Do you know what it's like to have nothing to do still sit at your desk for six more hours and pretend you are working? I can do a lot more than type up a letter and file papers that no one is going to look at ever again."

"Do Mom and Dad know?" I asked.

"Do you think they'd send you out here if they knew? They'd make me come home and as bad as things are I don't want to do that."

"Kate, I don't know what to say," I said.

"Well, what would you know? You just started college. Wait until you hit the real world. It isn't pretty." Even when everything was going wrong she could still find something hurtful to say to me and all I was doing was trying to help. I wanted to yell back at her, tell her I'm not her clueless little sister like she thinks I am but I couldn't do it. If our roles were reversed, Kate would have her comeback on the tip of her tongue. I had nothing.

"I don't know what to do next," she said.

These were the types of conversations I'd thought Kate and I would have when I was younger, but in my imagination, our roles were reversed. I had only rehearsed my lines, the younger sister looking for help from her perfect older sister. I never imagined the other side, trying to comfort her. She was the older sister. That was her job.

"The worst thing," she said, "is that I think Reginald is going to come back. Any minute he's just going to call me and tell me it was all a mistake. I can't do anything without having this stupid phone on me even though I know he is not going to call."

She took a step closer to the edge of the bridge and looked down.

"Twenty-five people a year kill themselves by jumping off this bridge," Kate said. "Very few survive."

"Kate what are you doing?" I asked. Kate couldn't be talking about doing that herself. Things weren't going well but this was my sister, this was Kate. She was undefeatable. She couldn't be thinking this.

"Don't worry. I'm still too afraid of heights to go anywhere near the edge. But I'm not saying I haven't thought about it." She took a step back.

"Kate, it's going to get better," I said. "I mean, it has to, right?"

"No, it doesn't have to," she said. "But it can't get worse."

This was the perfect place for me to bring up the great things about Kate that I thought of for my dream maid of honor speech. But without practice, without a real chance to prepare and with Kate right there in front of me my mind halted. It was my moment to help Kate, it could be the only time this would ever happen and I was frozen. All I needed was something good to say, some simple compliment, one thing she had ever done for me but I couldn't think of anything good. I could only remember the bad things, the times she "forgot" to pick me up at school and I walked home in the winter, when I had to miss my girl scout camping trip because the entire family had to go see Kate at cheerleading championships, how she couldn't even sit through my entire graduation ceremony even though I had attended everything she'd even done. Then I saw one of the blue signs.

"There is hope," I said.

Then I laughed. I didn't want to but I couldn't help it. And then I couldn't stop. Kate's face turned from despair to anger.

"What the hell are you laughing at? I'm miserable, my world is crashing down around me and you think this is funny?"

I clutched at my sides, still laughing, unable to speak. Finally, I pointed to the signs. Kate saw it but it took her a few seconds to register. Then she started laughing. That made me laugh louder and finally we both crumpled to the sidewalk in stitches.

"I'm so sorry," I said. "It's like the title of an after-school special."

"We should call the number and tell them the signs work, but maybe not exactly how they wanted them to," Kate said.

It took a few minutes, but we regained our composure then we shared an awkward hug. We weren't sure how to do it or how long to hold it so we held each other so long that we were both waiting for each other to let go.

"Thanks," she said. "Sometimes you just need a good laugh. Now let's finish this walk and go back to my apartment and get drunk on some cheap jug wine."

We walked faster and I could barely keep up with Kate. She had gone from mopey to energized and in no time, we were across the bridge. I took my camera out and took a picture looking back across the bridge then one of Kate with her arms held up in mock triumph. I handed her the

66

camera and she took one of me in the same pose. Then we turned and started walking back across.

"How long did it take us to get across?" Kate asked.

"Forty-five minutes not including the laughter and the hug," I said.

We settled into a comfortable pace on the way. We were walking against traffic and the headlights of the oncoming cars shined in our eyes. Kate walked next to the traffic and I walked on her left. The sun was all but gone and the lights of the city to our left were popping on one by one. A light cloud cover started to sneak in from the ocean. The sidewalk was nearly empty now except for the occasional cyclist headed across.

"Missy, look," Kate shouted. A man was trying to climb over the railing.

"That's the guy who took our picture," I said.

Kate ran towards him.

"What are you doing?" she said to him.

He climbed up the railing and reached for the vertical cables that ran down from the giant cable to the bridge deck. He lifted a work boot over the railing.

"Stop!" Kate yelled. He paid no attention to her. Kate reached for him and clamped onto his waist.

"Let go of me," he shouted.

"You shouldn't do this," she said.

"Get out of here," he shouted. He had a plain black cap atop his head and wore a brown workman's jacket and jeans with dirt splotches below the pockets. He wasn't a large man but should have been able to shake Kate off his arm. No matter how hard he tried to free himself Kate would not let go.

"Whatever it is it can't be that bad," Kate said. "It's going to get better."

The man used both hands to push Kate off and was free for a second but she just grabbed back onto him.

"Leave me alone. What is wrong with you?" the man

shouted. "Just let me do this."

"No way. My life sucks, too and I'm not jumping. There's no reason you should."

The man stopped for a second and stared at Kate. He eased up just a little bit.

"What is so bad about your life, pretty girl?" he asked.

"Well, I lost my job," Kate said. "And my boyfriend dumped me. By text! And it's Thanksgiving and my sister, who hates me, is the only person who came to visit me."

"I don't hate you," I said. Even if I did, I didn't want her to tell it to a stranger, even one we were trying to keep from jumping off a bridge.

"That's it," the man said. "That's the worst that happened to you? My wife left me. She took our daughter with her. I haven't worked in a year."

Kate stared him down. She looked over at me but I offered only a shrug. Going from bystander to involved party was not part of my makeup. I preferred to stay on the sidelines during situations like this. Kate looked flummoxed. She looked back at me, then back at the man, her hand still clinging to his arm

"Fine," she said. "Let's jump together." She let go of him and climbed up the railing.

"Kate, what the hell are you doing?" I shouted. I raced to the railing. Shivers shot through my body and my knees wobbled as I got closer to the edge. Kate stepped onto the middle rung then reached her hand out to the man. His face turned ashen. I stood behind them trying to figure out what she would do next. I wanted to just grab her and pull her back but I was afraid I'd accidentally send her over the edge.

"Are you ready?" she said.

The man didn't respond.

"It's over two hundred feet down," Kate said. "That's about five seconds. Just enough time to change your mind, but it will be too late. If we are lucky, the impact with the water will kill us, quick and easy, but that doesn't always happen. Sometimes you drown. And once we're in, who knows where our bodies will go. Sometimes they wash into the bay. Sometimes they get pulled out to the ocean. We could be shark food. We could get picked apart by birds. We could just wash up on a beach bloated from salt water."

The wind picked up and Kate steadied herself on the railing. The man remained still. He opened his mouth and touched his tongue to his lips. Their eyes locked on each other, neither blinking.

"Watch," she said. She reached into her pocket, pulled out her phone and tossed it off the bridge. It fell fast then disappeared into the water below.

"For now, let's pretend that phone was the cause of all of our problems."

They stood there. Neither moved.

"My name is Kate and this is my sister Melissa. We both don't want to be together right now, and neither of us wants to be on this bridge. But we decided to walk across the bridge together and we are almost done. Instead of jumping, why don't you walk with us the rest of the way?"

The man looked out over the railing. The traffic hummed as cars drove over the metal grates of the roadway. For a moment, it all blurred to the background and we were the only ones on that bridge. Finally, the man stepped away from the railing. His boots thumped on the sidewalk, then Kate stepped down, too. I exhaled. The man started walking and Kate placed herself between him and the railing. Each step felt like an eternity. I followed behind them. We walked in silence, the three of us, until the bridge ended and the road began to wind back down. The man turned to Kate.

"Thank you," he said. "It doesn't make it all better, but thank you."

"You're welcome," Kate said. He turned, gave us a quick look then continued walking.

Back at the car, Kate's hands shook as she tried to unlock the door. Droplets of sweat dripped down my face. Kate put the keys in the ignition but didn't start the car. I cracked my window open and we sat, our heavy breaths filling the car.

"That was intense," she said.

"You called me Melissa," I said.

"It was a serious situation. Missy is not a name for a serious situation."

"And five seconds?" I asked.

"High school physics problem," she said. "Don't worry," she said. "I'm still afraid of heights. There's no way I could climb over that railing to do anything."

"But you did climb the railing," I said.

She turned the key, the engine started and we pulled out of the parking spot and headed for Kate's apartment. The entire ride home Kate asked me questions about school, about boys, about San Diego, about when she could come visit me, about Mom and Dad, the kinds of conversations sisters are supposed to have but we never did. On Thanksgiving, we made one of the worst dinners we'd ever eaten and ended up at a diner eating open faced turkey sandwiches and sipping stale coffee. We spent the rest of the weekend roaming San Francisco. We ate in Chinatown, walked down Lombard Street, and snapped crab legs on the Embarcadero. We took a few pictures together and emailed them to our parents, but only the ones where we didn't smile. She still made fun of me every time I called it San Fran and she called me Missy, but it didn't bother me. I didn't open my books until she dropped me off at the airport on Sunday. She didn't mention Reginald, or her phone, or the bridge the rest of the weekend.

Sebastian's Sea Bass

"TEDDY, DARLING, this fish doesn't taste right," said Barbara.

"Well, we can't have that Babs," replied Theodore Van Horne to his new bride as he signaled to the Maître D'.

Van Horne, a well-known New York City multimillionaire, made his fortune in the rapidly expanding radio broadcasting business of the Roaring Twenties. He was important enough to bypass the waiter with complaints about the food.

"Yes Mr. Van Horne, how may I serve you?" asked Gregory, the tuxedo-clad Maître D'.

"Gregory, Mrs. Van Horne doesn't like the way her fish tastes."

"I am terribly sorry, Mrs. Van Horne," said Gregory, facing Barbara and bowing slightly. "May I inquire as to which fish dish you ordered?"

"Of course, it was Sebastian's Sea Bass."

"Very good, Mrs. Van Horne, I will go tell the chef immediately."

"No, I want to talk with him myself," said Van Horne sternly.

Gregory disappeared quickly behind the swinging double doors to the kitchen.

"I'm sorry Babs, I wanted everything to be perfect for our

honeymoon. The Stone Perch Hotel has an excellent reputation."

"Oh, Teddy, it has been wonderful," she replied, holding out her hand for him to grasp. "The Honeymoon suite, the Art Deco lobby. Look how romantic, we can see the moon reflected in the ocean from our table. I'll just order something else."

Van Horne didn't reply, releasing Barbara's hand as the chef approached their table. Chef Paul was dressed in traditional all-white French style with a high starched hat, double-breasted coat, a long kerchief, knotted at the neck, and a half apron cinched at the waist.

"Good evening. I am Chef Paul. My apologies that Madam is not pleased with the sea bass," said Paul with a French accent. "It is a new recipe."

"I have sampled it and find it has a displeasing aftertaste," said Van Horne.

"Perhaps too much Nepeta mint herb seasoning," replied Paul.

"Just take the dish away, mine too, we'll start over again. Lobster Thermidor for two, unless that is another new recipe," Van Horne said sarcastically.

"No, no Monsieur, the Thermidor is wonderful, excellent choice," replied Paul.

Gregory signaled for the waiter to remove the dinner plates as Paul turned to leave for the kitchen. "Chef Paul, wait just a minute," called out Van Horne. "Sebastian's Sea Bass? Who is Sebastian?"

"Yes, of course, Sebastian approves all my new fish recipes. I will have to scold him on this one," replied Paul.

"Rightfully so."

Paul nodded then continued to the kitchen.

"Teddy, Let's just enjoy the view," said Barbara looking out the window over the stone balcony to the ocean. "Oh, look. What a beautiful calico cat."

"That's Sebastian, Chef Paul's cat," said the waiter

clearing the table.

"Sebastian's a cat!" said Van Horne.

Barbara looked at him, brightening her face while raising her eyebrows, and smiled. They both laughed.

Van Horne shook his head. "Let's have some more Champagne."

"A toast to Sebastian," said Barbara. "Let's hope his next choice is better than his last."

Birdsong

AS THE TWIGS TUMBLED from the old Aspen in the garden, they scooped them off the ground in their beaks and stuck them into the ever-growing tangle. They thought that nobody saw them, but I did - every time they hopped over to the hole in the bottom of the tree-stump. That's where they live, I told Mum, that's where they keep their sticks. She smiled, without her eyes smiling, and picked up her red-stained glass. That's silly, she said after her long swig, birds don't keep sticks. They fly and they sing. And when they don't fly or sing, they aren't birds anymore.

I wanted them to be birds.

I visited their hole. I saw their home inside; there were more birds than I thought there would be. I'd only seen two of them - hopping around with their red bellies close to the ground, combing through yellowed leaves and blades of grass, but there were more in the tree-stump. Three little ones, huddled to the side while the bigger ones poked at their tangle. The littlest birds screamed, but that's not singing. I took one and tried to make it fly.

It didn't.

I guess it wasn't a bird anymore.

Dad told me that I shouldn't be touching filthy animals. He said they have diseases, and that I shouldn't be so dirty, covering myself in mud and meddling with garden pests. I told him that they aren't pests, they're my friends.

My cheek hurt.

I saw them again. I was told to disappear until dinner, and stop staring, it's creepy. I went to see how big their tangle was. I sat on the tree-stump, swinging my head between my legs to see the four little upside-down birds sitting neatly together. I watched their mouths open to scream. Maybe they were saying hello. I asked them will you sing for me?

They didn't sing for me.

They didn't fly either.

Maybe they weren't birds anymore.

I told Mum when she came home. I told her the birds aren't singing. They're not flying either. Are they birds anymore? She told me I'm tired, go away. I don't care about your dumb birds.

So maybe they were still birds.

All four birds were hopping around, picking at moss and twigs through the sludge of fallen leaves. I wondered if the little ones missed their brother. I wanted to call back to Mum, ask her if the birds were still birds, but I didn't think she would help me. She's too tired to care about you, I told the birds, but I'm still here. Even though you're not birds anymore.

Mum would want me to help you, because you're not birds anymore.

As the twigs tumbled from the old Aspen in the garden, I found a big rock. I knew that they were only filthy animals, dumb birds that weren't birds anymore. They wouldn't hurt the way I did. It would be okay.

I helped the birds fly again.

I helped them sing.

A Man and His Best Friend

I WAS PACKING my suitcase that laid on top of the bed we used to share. I had just told my wife that I didn't love her anymore. This had become a special skill I had acquired after rushing many times into relationships that I never intended to stick with. I had always said the things they wanted to hear to make them believe that I was going to be around forever, but I knew fully well that wasn't true. By the sounds of her screams and crying in the other room, this time was no different. I wasn't alone though, in a room that once shared many emotions, but was now empty, cold, and meaningless, my truest companion sat by my side. Of course, I only met him through my soon to be divorcée, but he showed me a side of things I could have never discovered on my own. Through the downfall of our relationship, the ugliest of the ugly, my new friend brought joy to me, surprisingly more joy than any of the women I've let down before ever have. As my suitcase of belongings got fuller, and I debated between what items truly belonged to me and what items were even worth keeping, I realized there was nothing of sentimental value I could possibly want to take with me, I felt relieved this was all over but at the same time I hated myself for wasting two full years when I could've been exploring the world, or making a name for myself, or at the very least enjoying a damn cold beer with my friends.

I won't miss a single thing in this entire room, not the bed where we spent so many nights not even talking, let alone touching each other. It's like our fingertips had turned ice cold and one touch could freeze the other person solid. That bed should burn, and rot away in the vast hells of the worlds failed relationships. The squeaking springs will haunt me inside my mind, a personal token to take with me, I guess. My clothes barely fit inside my suitcase at this point, so I decide to leave a few behind, maybe this will be like leaving my mark, although I'm sure she will burn it the moment she finds it. I'm sure my pal won't mind having some of these things around, for now at least. I sure won't miss the damned TV, and definitely not the self manufactured antenna that comes along with it. Five channels isn't enough for any couple to pretend that they still love each other, the repetitive shows really exposed the lack of conversation the two of us were able to inspire on our own.

At this point my wife was in the kitchen, hunting for her keys, as usual. She could never find a damned thing, I was her private detective for personal belongings. Really, truly am not going to miss that. She glanced at me as she headed for the door, a look of disgust, but I could tell she was sad behind her painted emotions. This was a turning of the chapter for her as well. I didn't react, I just pressed my lips against each other and gave her a nod, expressionless. The door slammed and I was finally alone, well, just me and my buddy that is. This was my time to look through everything and see if I could find any last minute items to stash in a bag before I left. I went through some old records, none of which I felt any connection to. I left them on the shelf where I found them so they could resume collecting dust. I then made my way to the liquor cabinet. A few bottles of wine could come in handy, definitely would be a whole lot easier to forget this hell hole of an apartment. I stashed two bottles of red wine in a bag designated for the rest of the alcohol l had already claimed. There was a bottle of bourbon already opened, and since no one came to my going away party, I guess I'll just have to celebrate my send off on my own. I poured myself a glass and toured the apartment one last time, reminiscing of all the memories that were created, and replaying the entire self made movie titled Our Lives in this Shithole Apartment from start to finish in my head. I laughed to myself and moved back to the bedroom. I took one last look, to make sure if there's anything I do need that I'm not forgetting it behind because I won't have the courage to come back here and pick it up from her. It seems as if I have everything I need and there's not much more reason for me to stand around in this ex-living space any longer.

I moved all of my belongings to the front hall, lined them up accordingly, seeing as though it would probably take me a few trips to my car in order to get everything down. As I carried a couple boxes and one suitcase down the hall to the elevator, I was stopped by several people who found my departure a bit of a shock. They all wished me well and hoped that we would maybe cross paths again someday, I hoped that wasn't true. I didn't particularly like any of my neighbours, they all seemed too friendly and way too nosy for my likings. I would have liked them better if I didn't know them at all. But I guess my wishes have come true, and these final passes, to and from the elevator would be my final laps. One of the trips I was even a little spontaneous and took the stairs, something in all of the two years I had lived there I had never done, and by the time I had reached the top I had understood why that was. The last trip I would take would conclude with me not having to come back, ever. So this was it, this was everything I had wanted at one point in time, and now I've done a complete one-eighty and am going the other direction. Would I feel happier once I left? Would I feel that intangible weight lift from my shoulders and be ready to start a new chapter? I wasn't really sure, but it felt as right as right could feel. I stood in the frame of the door, taking my time analyzing everything I was leaving behind, there was just one last thing to do. Standing no further than two feet away from me was my pal, my best friend. His ears were perked up, his eyes were wide, and his tail was wagging. He had no clue what was about to happen, he was just happy to see me, as he always was. I bent down, and put my face close to his, I rubbed the top of his head for the last time and whispered softly to him, "I'm going to miss you buddy."

He just stared at me. His eyes looking as deep as ever, my eyes starting to water, but of course he didn't know what that really meant. To him this felt like no different than all the other times I walked out that door and returned only a few hours later to his loving kisses. This time I was walking out the door and never coming back, and he would wait there, patiently, until the day I returned. I closed the door, and the sound of the lock turning felt like misery. I slid the key under the door and could hear him walk up to it. He knew I was still there, and I put my hand close to the crack at the bottom, I could feel his warm breath on my fingertips, I stood up and walked away. This is what real heartbreak feels like.

Erin's Summit

ERIN PLACED ONE FOOT on the hill and lost her balance. It angered a flock of geese and they flapped their wings sending loose feathers into the air. The feathers floated down, and she thought of the day they covered her mountain climbing partner's coffin with dirt.

Someone looked down from the top of the hill. Erin looked away and her hand shook when she remembered Johan's face while he slid past her on K2. Her hand reached out for him but grasped only snow. They found his body farther down the mountain. She never knew who helped her down that day, but nobody would help her up now.

The person on the hill vanished. A gust of wind blew the feathers away like her dream of becoming the first woman to summit all fourteen 8000-meter mountains.

She walked away from the hill and knew there would be no summit today. At home, she sat on the deck.

The next-door neighbor started decorating for a party. They didn't care about social distancing. No one around here feared the virus now. It would be a long night. They never invited her, but they did invite her ex-husband Drew who lied to everyone saying she was insane. They believed him since she spent time in a mental hospital after the accident, he never added the part about him cheating on her.

She avoided the windows afraid they would see her shadow then she heard Drew's voice.

"Crazy, sick, don't trust her, maybe she killed that mountain climber," then the worst. "She should be put away again."

The words cut deeper than a knife. She peeked out. None of them wore a mask.

Some of the neighbors at the party mumbled agreement. One voice proclaimed, "Let's shun her. She should wear a mask all the time."

"I heard she is infected now." She wasn't.

She slammed the window shut and glanced out as all the heads turned in her direction. She ducked down but they knew she was there. It confirmed his words. They would avoid her even more now.

As the music and voices got louder, she jumped when a scratching came from the back door. Someone was breaking in. She grabbed a knife and crept toward the door. When she looked out, nobody was there. She opened the door and a stray cat walked in.

"What do you want?"

The cat jumped up on the couch.

"Are you sure you want to stay here?"

The cat looked at her then curled up on the couch.

"We'll I guess cats are not contagious."

Someone laughed when she walked into the kitchen.

The music blared from the party. She walked through the house ducking under the windows. Feeling like a prisoner, she got in the car and drove to a hill she practiced on when she started mountain climbing. When the sand road ended, she walked down the fire trail. A sad owl hooted in the distance. The hill looked like a mountain.

A few steps up the trail and she hyperventilated. She took her mask off. The dream of mountain climbing again faded away.

Panic set in when she saw a man standing on the

summit. She fell backward and rolled to the bottom of the hill.

"No." The voice came from the top of the hill and it wasn't a man. It was a girl.

She waited, but the hill remained silent and threatening. She shivered and hurried back to the truck. Sand flew out from behind the wheels like a wake behind a speedboat when she left. The party still lit up her backyard. Unable to sleep, she put on the television. A station flashed a picture of a girl. A lady with tears running down her face talked into a microphone. "Please help me find my girl."

"The girl's voice." It could be her on the hill.

She called the number on the screen. A lady answered, listened to her, then cut her off.

"I heard a girl's voice."

"We can't follow up on a voice in the woods." They asked her name and said they would call back.

"Also, there's people not social distancing."

"Is that why you really called?"

"No." She hung up and put her phone on the charger.

After an hour, she couldn't wait anymore. They might have looked up her name and thought she was crazy. She dashed out the door.

Halfway to the hill, she realized that her cell phone was still on the charger.

At the base of the hill, every shadow became a threat. She tripped and pain seared through her ankle.

When she got up, she heard a girl crying. The hill loomed before her like a wall. She picked up a broken branch and struggled up the hill using it as a cane. The girl's sobbing drove her upward.

Without looking back, she reached the edge of the summit. She noticed an outline of a person. The man looked like a giant when he stood up while a smaller shadow moved inside the tent.

The man lifted a bottle to his mouth. She smelled the

whiskey and hoped that he was drunk. She crawled toward the tent. The man entered it and the girl cried out.

Erin picked up the branch and opened the tent flap. The man looked up and dropped the girl. Erin swung the branch, and it broke against his face. The recoil knocked her backward. The girl screamed, and the man came out of the tent with streaks of blood across his face.

"I'll kill you." He lumbered toward her.

Erin crawled backward and moved toward the edge of a cliff. The man charged her. She moved sideways at the last minute and he tumbled over the edge and disappeared. A splash echoed through the woods. She couldn't move and her hands trembled until the girl sobbed in the tent. Erin ran over and opened the flap. She was relieved to see the girl was okay and even wore a mask.

"Chloe?"

She nodded and started to cry.

"It's okay." Erin hugged her and led her to the path going down the hill, but first, she looked over the cliff and saw a fast-moving creek. There was no sign of the man. Chloe sobbed and collapsed. Erin helped her up and they hurried down the hill. Every sound and shadow became a threat. They kept going until they reached the truck. Chloe shivered in the passenger seat. Erin grasped her hand and held onto it as she drove straight to the ranger station. She held the girl's hand as they burst into the door.

The ranger jumped up, "What's going on?"

Erin pointed at Chloe, "The missing girl."

The people in the station gathered around the girl while Erin slipped out the door.

* * *

The party still went on as Erin walked past the windows. This time she didn't duck down. She collapsed on the couch and the cat rubbed against her.

83

"I guess you're staying with me now. Do you know I might be crazy?"

The cat purred.

"I guess you don't care. Do you like the name, Chloe?"

The cat snuggled against her. "Okay, Chloe, it is."

The next morning, Chloe's parents appeared on TV. "We want to thank the person who saved Chloe. She wants to see her." They said there was no trace of the man found in the creek or surrounding land.

Erin walked outside and the stench of beer met her. Next door, the trash cans overflowed with bottles and a few crows fought for food scraps on the ground while a few men snored on lounge chairs. They were oblivious to anything going on around them. She yelled out. "Good morning. I hope you all take COVID tests. Drew is infected." The men scrambled to their feet and looked at each other with fear in their eyes. She laughed out loud and hoped they suffered from hangovers.

Erin returned to the hill. After the police cleared the scene it looked empty and the only sound came from birds in the area. The hill looked smaller.

With a crooked stick, she struggled up the slope. She reached the summit and lifted the branch into the air. She went back down and climbed up again doing it over and over as fear and anger slipped away from her. The last time up, she stood on the summit and let out a yell. A few crows took flight and cawed back as she smiled and went back down then called the expedition leader for a mountain climbing team getting ready to go to Mt. Everest when the pandemic was over. She wondered if she could take a cat with her.

Eargasm

I SAT IN THE RECLINER, looking down the hall into the kitchen. I stared at the mustard yellow wall mount phone and the tangled cord that unfortunately could not reach this far. My heavy gaze was not helping the phone to ring. Oh, how I wish it would. Paula had said she'd call me back. That was 5 minutes ago. What could be going on in her house? Was she just toying with me? The phone rang. It sounded like a pop gun blast in my ears. I dashed to the phone to discover it was Aunt Jane calling to chat with my Mom. That was sure to tie-up the phone for at least twenty minutes, only to be interrupted for dinner. I told Aunt Jane that we were getting ready to sit down to dinner, and Mom would have to call her back. I reentered the living room. Toby had taken my chair.

"Good work, son," Dad said.

I shifted my eyes about the room. I thought I was about to be busted or oddly complimented for the cockroach prank I pulled on Mrs. Goodwin, my 5th-hour Trigonometry teacher. What else could he be talking about? In my defense, it was just a dead cockroach in her coffee. But she had looked like she was going to faint or puke, Paula and Joan took her to the nurse's office. I'd been waiting for hellfire to rain down from Sweetgum County High ever since. Every phone call could be a

85

blessing or a beating. I had to stand guard on that phone.

"When she gets on the phone with Jane, it sets dinner back 20 minutes," Dad said.

Good, Dad was an unwitting ally in keeping the phone free from Mom's grease smeared hands. Time slid by like a slug on a rug. Why wasn't she calling? Mom hollered out for me to set the table. I put a bowl of buttered brussels sprouts by Toby's chair. It was his favorite vegetable. We had them weekly. Dad started to complain one night. Go Dad, but Mom shut him down with an alarming look. I loaded up on the Kraft Mac 'n Cheese and steak. I was a growing boy. I needed to eat heartily and do my pushups to keep in shape for the Sweetgum swim team. Right when I had a mouthful of Mac 'n Cheese, the phone rang. I jumped up, but my Mom told me to get my keister in the seat, mister. It was a family rule, no answering the phone during dinner. We had to make the rule due to the night Dad answered a call from a solicitor. Toby and I had learned a couple new curse words from that call.

After Toby finished helping Mom with the dishes, he was in my ear whining about his seat. I played deaf. I hadn't complained when he claimed the chair from me after being out of it for 5 minutes.

"Go play, I'm watching the news with Dad," I said.

It was good to keep Dad in play on my side. Things often fell to Toby's way because he was the youngest. I was so tired of the, "because you're older, you should know better" line from Mom. I didn't give leave of the putrid green Barcalounger until Mom came in to retire from the kitchen. The dinner grease was like a lotion; she rubbed into her hands that would be chapped; otherwise, thanks to the daily washing-up. I slinked over to the phone, feeling a little guilty for not giving Aunt Jane's message to Mom. Aunt Jane called twice a day since her and Uncle Roger's divorce. You could always hear my cousins breaking each other's necks in the background.

I took up a position, reclined against the wall, waiting for the phone to ring. Toby picked up on my phone monitoring. He tried to think up a reason to use the phone.

"Mom, I need to call Ernie," he said.

"No, you don't. You'll see Ernie at school tomorrow," she said.

Toby stomped off and returned with a baseball bat. He started swinging it in the open kitchen.

"Toby, what the hell are you doing?" Dad said.

"I'm practicing for the spring tryouts," Toby said.

"Bullshit," I said.

"Language," Mom said.

Toby started to swing too close. I buckled down just to miss his swing. But the phone wasn't so lucky. The phone was in my lap with a plastic splinter tucked in my feathered bangs. When Dad got done reaming Toby, I implored him to fix the phone. I was willing to risk a phone call from Principal Dankworth if the phone would just ring from Paula.

"I can't. It's broke. When I get to the office tomorrow, I'll call Southwestern Bell. They'll send someone out with a new phone."

"Oh, Butch, get an Avocado one," Mom said.

The next day at school had to explain to Paula about the phone. I was worried she was going to shut me down.

"No, worries, Heath. I forgot all about it."

I was back at square one. That darn phone better be fixed when I get home. Because what I wanted to say, I didn't want to say it in the open halls. If you're gonna get rejected, it's better to do it in your own kitchen than the school cafeteria.

Mom was frowning at the Yellow Mustard phone on the wall.

"I said Avocado. They said they didn't get to pick the color. Well, who the hell does?" Mom said to me, and she went to the liquor cabinet for her afternoon sherry.

Toby was determined to unearth the reasons for my sudden phone obsession. He crouched by my feet, trying to tickle me through my tube socks. I shooed him away. But he stayed, and we drew Mom's attention.

"What's going on in there," Mom hollered. Mom was always hollering when she wanted to communicate. She was either hollering over the hiss of a frying pan or the too-loud volume of the TV.

I banged the back of my head on the wall. I couldn't get peace at school or at home. Why did the phone have to be hung in the kitchen, the social hub of the house? Oh, that was why. Well, it made it hard to flirt. Paula was in the Drama club, so I had to wait until 4:30 for her to get home. This time I had a secret weapon. I got my friend Jenny to start a rumor that I was an excellent kisser. I hoped it made it as far as Paula.

* * *

I put on my purple short shorts, blue-striped tube socks, a Cardinals ringer tee, and my white Converse Chucks. This was my best look. Paula invited me over after 8:30 p.m. because the kids would be in bed, and the Wilkersons wouldn't return until midnight. It was only 6 blocks, so I rode my bike over. I was just two months from a driver's license. My Mom said she didn't know who was more excited about the pending license, her or me. When I got my permit, she started listing all the errands I could take off her plate. I kinda wondered if she thought I would be cutting class for the full-time job of family chauffeur. Wouldn't it be great to have a note from my Mom everyday excusing me from class?

I followed Paula into the large kitchen. They had an Amana microwave on the kitchen counter. These people must be rich. Paula pulled out the pan and lid. She loaded it with oil and kernels. As Paula shook the popping pan, I fantasized about asking her to be my girlfriend. If someone as popular as Paula was your girlfriend, you could get any girl you wanted. Paula stared at me. Oh, shit, did I say any of that out loud?

"Hey, you're spacing out," she said. "Paying attention to a girl is rule number one for dating." I wanted to ask, but I didn't want to look dumb. Was there a rule book? It sure would make things easier. But it would kill the 'I didn't know' excuse. She started talking again. I ran my fingers through my feathered bangs and felt a cluster of pimples where the phone rests at the ear. It was Mom's greasy fingers on the phone receiver. She sure did grease up the new telephone awfully fast. I brushed my hair forward over my left ear to disguise the phone acne. We ate the whole bowl of popcorn, including the widows, left at the bottom. I leaned in for a kiss, and we were making out, heavy. Paula pushed me back to come up for air. She changed the channel to a rerun of Mr. Ed. I did not know what to think of that. I was ready for another round of make-out when she put her left pinky finger in her ear and twisted it like we had just come out of a pool of water. Then she stuck her pinky in her mouth.

Innocence Lost

MY SQUIRREL.....still.....lifeless.....it haunts me. I can smell the freshly turned field. The sun, warming my skin. The screams, they echo inside my head. I'm afraid. Loneliness envelops me. I'm aware I'm not alone. It all starts spinning. It's like a film strip with chunks cut out and then spliced together. I'm in a bathtub. I'm holding my breath underwater. Daddy is timing me. Just when I'm about to pass out from suffocating, I'm allowed to breathe. My head is pounding. I'm so nervous. All I can see are spots. He's screaming. All I want is to be loved. ... Fast forward.... I'm on the ground. Silent. Still. Not breathing. I aim my rifle at the target. There's a little orange sticker on the site so I can line it up. I can only blink or breathe in between shots. It was a lot for a little girl. My dad was an army ranger sniper with severe PTSD. I was taught young to be ready, aware and alert. Don't think just do. I was shown how to sneak up on animals. To be patient, diligent and silent. I would labor my breathing just like he taught me. No longer had I the innocence of a child. After catching him many times, I named him Charlie. I have now went full circle. I'm back at the beginning. He was to be a lesson not a pet. He didn't deserve to die. Not this way.

The Office

"THE RISE OF MENTAL HEALTH problems in men have come to the attention of the New Minister of Health who looks to stamp out the problem." The morning news stated as I was eating my cereal, drowned in milk making it soggy and unappetizing, that was trying to evade the spoon. This was the fourth time, in as many weeks, I had been fed this information, from the morning bulletin, before going to work and there had still been no attempt to 'stamp out the problem'. This didn't affect me, although, it was making me stressed. I finished the bowl of cereal, picked up my blazer, which brushed up the chair making my hand tremor, and jetted towards the door.

The walk to the office is the best moment of my day. Always. I feel free, can understand what life is, and come to terms with my senses. The cool air which scrapes my nose and the smell of nature ruptures my nostrils. This is how to live. The harsh sounds of birds penetrate my eardrums and the taste of what I had just eaten, for breakfast, is still fresh; yet fading away, as all good things do, as I stroll through the streets of what I was once proud to call my town. This is no town of mine now, it is a landfill infested with rats. They are everywhere: governing us, helping us and working with us. But I need to work so I continue to live here. After a swift half an hour walk, which I always do in fifteen minutes, I am facing the beige office block of my employers.

As I walk into the office, rubbing the cold, green mucus on the back of my rough goose-bumped hand, I look at the same old grey panels on the ceiling which suck the life out of them, already, dead. The same faces smiling behind computers; bobbing up to see who is there, just enough to suffice their nosiness. "It's just me" I cheerily say as I walk to the back of the room; getting sniggers of acknowledgement as I always do when I say that, probably just to insinuate 'aw bless we must humour him'.

As I looked to the back of the room; my desk awaited with a mound of paper perched on top of it. This was odd. The company usually emails the work I need to do, usually just dealing with wingy emails from customers and working on a website I don't even care about. I must do a good job though, otherwise, I will lose my job. The job I once loved but now hate.

I work through the day, no problem, swiftly; meaning I can have a long well earned break at the end of the shift. I am the only one who skips dinner to do this. After I finish for my break I stand up and look busy while I look for someone to talk to. No one. They're all working. I walk back, head down, to my desk which has a computer and start scrolling through whatever web pages I want that aren't restricted. After five wholesome minutes; I'm bored. I look away from the grey, dull desktop and slouch my face into my hands. I can feel water flooding my eyes, yet I can't cry. I won't cry. This is just stress and I need to face it. I sit for the last hour, which feels like ten, holding my head and occasionally standing up to stretch, in pain. A headache, it must be from work, I'm just tired.

The clock, finally, hits five and I stand. A little bit wobbly on my feet, I quickly sit down again as a blackout of blood gushes to my feet, which is followed by a fountain of pain. I stand, successfully this time and walk, the fastest

I have walked today, to the door and open it. Now for the worst bit of the day: the walk back home. All I see is beams of orange lights paving the way through the darkness, which I'd rather be in. The chill freezes my hands and toes and all I can hear are chavs shouting, penetrating my eardrums. I walk fast, faster than this morning, and get home to my empty house in ten minutes. I unlock the door and stagger in throwing my blazer into the lounge while I heat up what was supposed to be eaten hours ago.

Once the bell pings from the microwave, I immediately open the door, grab a fork and take the plastic container of mush into the lounge, burning my fingers and making my hands scream. I throw myself onto the sofa, place the dish on my lap, making my thighs cry out, and put on the television with the remote I left and the chair this morning. The news plays: "Mental health problems are on the rise in men so we're going to be talking to a counsellor about how to identify if you need help." I look down, take a forkful of the slimy, mush, which does taste even worse than it looks, and look back, noticing I've missed all the other stories. And there the counsellor is, sat on the sofa talking.

"If you have any of these problems at home, you need to see someone and tell them how you're feeling." The counsellor patronises and continues with the list. "Uncontrollable headaches when not doing anything..." I have that. "Stress or feeling anxious" Yes. "Constantly feeling tired." Oh no! "Feeling teary when doing nothing." I have all of them but I'm not a psycho.

I need help!

Violence

SHE SAT IN THE BUS and embraced the rare sun rays in the grey city of London as soon as they touched her skin. She felt the warmth. She felt how the sun rays flooded the roads, right into the window of the bus. The sun always made her feel better. The brightness of it seems to take the darkness inside of her away. Right now, all she wanted was to rest in that sunshine. Allow herself to feel all the positive things she never allowed herself to feel: Peace, tranquillity, happiness. What she felt reminded her of Springtime. It was the same feeling of excitement she felt, seeing the first sun rays of the year, melting the snow off the branches of a tree. The same excitement she felt when she saw the first crops after the trees have been covered in snow. Almost as though she was in love. The first warmth. The excitement for growth.

She was putting together the pieces again. Collecting the shards of the heart that had been broken. How did she let this happen? How did her emotions spin into a force as destructive as a hurricane? Into words as sharp as lightning? Into screams as loud as thunder? Into beatings that swept her away like egre?

She remembered the hits like striking waves that almost drowned her to death. She could feel the strokes around her neck again, the shortness of breath trying to gasp for

94

air. She remembered the taste of fear on her tongue. It was all too familiar.

She remembered blood. She remembered nightmares that were never dreams and horrific scenes where she was starring in. She remembered playing the same role over and over again.

"I was just playing a role" she said to herself. She shook it off, embraced the sun and knew she could never let it go.

Violence has become a part of her now.

Nightmares

"THE TRICK IS in the honey," Evan said, as he handed me a mug filled with warm tea. He gently sat down next to me, placing himself under the covers. Grabbing my hand, he squeezed it softly, a reassuring smile resting on his face. "It was just a nightmare, it's okay."

"I know," I said before taking a sip from the mug, the warmth filling my stomach. It soothed me of my tension; I dropped my shoulders, feeling myself relax. He was right. It was all just a nightmare, nothing more.

I smiled at him, placing the mug on the nightstand before cuddling next to him. The nightmare had been ingrained into my memories, having had it every night at the same time without fail. The image of the woman opening the door and creeping into the room replayed itself in my head.

"Do you want to go back to sleep now?" Evan asked as he hugged my waist. I nodded, closing my eyes. His snores filled the room within seconds of the light turning off. But, I stayed up, unable to sleep, paralyzed with fear.

I could hear the door slowly creak open.

AUTHOR BIOGRAPHIES

RACHAEL BIGGS
Eleven Days 'til Sunday

Rachael Biggs is an author and screenwriter whose memoir *Yearning for Nothings and Nobodies* was published in 2012. She studied creative writing at Langara College and UCLA and holds a screenwriting diploma from Vancouver Film School. Her short fiction has appeared in *The Dalhousie Review, Door is a Jar, Charge* and *Adelaide Magazines* among others. Her first feature film *Kill Me* is in development with Straight Arrow Films in Venice, California.

KIMBERLEY BLACK DAY
Innocence Lost

Kimberly Black Day
is a country girl from
a small town in
Southeastern Indiana.
Growing up in her
beloved countryside
home, she spent
much of her time
writing about her
fantasies as only she
could dream.
Sometimes these
thoughts came to her
in the woods or when
searching the fields
for arrowheads, a

favorite past time she relished. Her first two poems were
published by Train River Publishing in the spring and
summer of 2020 in anthologies. One day she hopes to write
her story. This is the beginning one flashback at a time.

ALAN BRYANT
Sketching

Alan Bryant lives in Mumbles, South Wales, conveniently situated between the bus stop, the chip shop and the castle he looks up at in awe every day.

He has won the National Writers' Groups Historical short story prize and had many short stories accepted for anthologies. He has read his work on BBC Radio Wales and somehow gained a BA in Creative Writing and Literature with the Open University.

His first attempt at self publishing is a 'how to' Amazon ebook on house buying - *The Householders' Guide To Sanity*. This has not made him rich.

Alan started writing his first novel with a quill pen until hiding it in a drawer when he realised he needed to make a living. He maintains it is almost finished.

ROBERT DOMINICK
Home Team

Rob Dominick has been writing since the 4th grade, and has carried that love of language into a career in English education. He holds a Master's Degree from Villanova University, and has taught in the Philadelphia area for the last 14 years. In his spare time, he enjoys playing the guitar and watching films, two of his other lifelong loves. Rob started his IG poetry account, @realrobdompoetry, in January 2020, and plans on publishing his first poetry collection within the next year.

WILLIAM FALO
Erin's Summit

William Falo studied environmental science in college and lives in South Jersey with his family including a papillon named Dax. His fiction has appeared or is forthcoming in *Vamp Cat Magazine*, *Fictive Dream*, *Litro Magazine*, *Fragmented Voices*, the Australian charity anthology *Burning Love* and other literary journals. He was nominated for a Pushcart Prize. You can find him on Twitter @williamfalo and Instagram @william.falo

SARA FAROOQI
The Crater

Sara Farooqi is a London-based writer, illustrator and musician. As a child with an overactive imagination, she was drawing and writing as soon as she could hold a pencil and had a poem published in a children's anthology at the age of ten. She began playing the cello at the age of seven and pursued a path in music, studying Music at Goldsmiths University of London. She began a career in the music industry, but then chose to follow her true passion - writing. She is currently working on completing her first collection of poetry, to be released later this year. She is also writing her first novel alongside a collection of short stories. Her work weaves between themes of love, lust, trauma, her colourful family and upbringing and her unusual dreams and nightmares.

LUCY GARDNER
When the Storm Ends

Lucy Gardner is a native Sandlapper who teaches sixth-grade English by day and binge reads the literary world by night. She also skydives, drives a little too fast, and off-roads in her Jeep with a bunch of friends who probably won't read this story.

ALEXIS HUNTER
Tiny God

Alexis Hunter is 39 years old and lives in County Durham, North East England. She writes short stories of many genres, and has previously featured in *Who Writes Short Shorts?*, *Twist in Time Magazine* and *VSS 365 Anthology: Volume One*.

In December 2017 she published her first children's picture book, *Clara's Search for Magic*.

Her other interests include painting (terribly), photography (slightly less terribly), and petting animals (with their permission, of course).

CHARLOTTE KERWICK
For the Joy of Panda Tiles

Charlotte is an unrepentant slattern who has written in obscurity for the last 40 years. She views her subjects through the lavender lens of a manic-depressive, underachiever.

In 2014, Charlotte began writing haiku during her daily commute. Hundreds of haiku later, she branded this persona, "The Existential Commuter". The serendipitous meeting of Charlotte and her soon to be illustrator/collaborator, Elise Mari Clare, at the Algonquin, no less - led to the birth of a creative, soul-sister partnership. Shortly after, Charlotte began reading her haiku and other poetry at open mics around NYC.

Existential Commuter illustrated haiku appear in the *Train River Poetry: Summer 2020* anthology and their upcoming COVID Anthology. Charlotte is proud that Train River is also the first to publish one of her short stories. Charlotte's other talents include marathon napping and embracing financial oblivion.

Charlotte is the daughter of the late, award-winning, Jersey poet, Max Greenberg. She lives in NJ with her enormously supportive and irritating, husband and son and their three cats, Paige, Edgar and Tito.

FRANK KOZUSKO
Sebastian's Sea Bass

Frank Kozusko is a retired US Navy submarine officer and nuclear engineer. After the Navy, he spent 20 years as a university professor of mathematics. Third beat: Writer.

Frank writes poetry and short stories across many genres. He favors sci-fi and mystery stories influenced by his boyhood fascination with TV programs like "The Twilight Zone", "Perry Mason", and "Alfred Hitchcock Presents."

His online publications include: "Merry River" in *Bewildering Stories*, "The Pallbearer" in *Ariel Chart*, "The Grandfather Clock" in *Literally Stories*, "Death in the Dust" in *Over My Dead Body*.

His print publications include: "The Snowman's Hat" in *Pilcrow & Dagger*, "Boy on a Bicycle" in *The Avalon Literary Review*.

His anthologized publications include: "A Steak and a Story" in *Bubble Off Plumb*, "Circadian Rhythms" in *The Twofer Compendium*, "Links" in *Paradox: The Inner Circle Writers' Group Crime/Mystery/Thriller Anthology 2019*.

His self-published poetry collections include: *Boomer Bounce: Poems on a Generation* and *Thoughts That Surface: Poems of a Silent Service Cold Warrior*.

He wrote the children's picture book *Can Penguins Fly?*
Frank can be reached at circadianrs@yahoo.com.

LISA MARIE LOPEZ
The Flowers that Changed Him

Lisa Marie Lopez resides in sunny northern California with her husband and two box turtles. She loves baseball, reading, the blue sky, and spending time writing fiction in cozy cafes. She's had many short stories and flash fiction pieces published in a variety of anthologies and literary journals. Some of these include: *Blink-Ink*, *The Ocotillo Review*, and *Molecule: A Tiny Lit Mag.*

ELLA MEASEY
Birdsong

Raised (not born) on the Isle of Wight, Ella Measey is doing her best to emerge into the writing scene, hoping to entertain audiences with her unique, charmingly unnerving style. She enjoys short prose, but is building a reputation online as an Instagram poet.

ALEXA NOHEMI
Nightmares

Alexa Nohemi is a young writer, poet, and author of the short story, "Nightmares". Since childhood, Alexa had been an avid reader which sparked her curiosity in writing and creating stories full of thrillers, mysteries, and worlds with adventure around every corner. When she's not writing, she is baking, studying, or spending time with her family.

RUTH ISABELLA PETERS
Violence

Born in Germany with a Nigerian background, author Ruth Isabella Peters reflects diversity.

The London-based writer holds multiple degrees in a range of subjects, including Criminology and Psychology, as well as International Security from renowned King's College. After her academic career, her passion for writing has taken over. Now, she combines her academic knowledge with past experiences to create introspective short stories. In her writings, Peters speaks on personal hardships and raises awareness of mental health, domestic abuse and grief.

Her profound writing style is food for thought.

As a mentor, coach and writer, Peters is the voice of a generation whose struggles are unheard of.

For more content, follow:

Instagram: @ruthisabellaa
Medium: Ruth Isabella Peters

LEAH SACKETT
Eargasm

Late summer 2020, Leah Holbrook Sackett will publish her debut book of short stories with *REaDLips Press.* Leah is an adjunct lecturer in the English department at the University of Missouri - St. Louis, where she also earned her M.F.A. Her stories explore journeys toward autonomy and the boundaries placed on the individual by society, family, and self. Specifically, Leah enjoys the rich genre of Coming of Age stories. Learn about her published fiction at LeahHolbrookSackett.website

MATTHEW SANCHE
A Man and His Best Friend

Matthew Sanche is a young new writer from Toronto, Ontario, Canada. 'A Man and His Best Friend' is his first published short story. His passion for writing was inspired by many great authors long before his generation. He believes the written word can be more powerful than the spoken. Along with fiction, Matthew also writes poetry, and has been published by Train River Publishing before, under the pen name Matthew John Poetry.

MIKE SMOLAREK
Across The Golden Gate

Mike Smolarek lives in Riverside, Illinois, just outside of Chicago. He has been published in *Two With Water* and in the book *Daddy Cool*, an anthology of writing by and for dads edited by Ben Tanzer. He has been part of several reading series, including Two With Water/Curbside Splendor and Essay Fiesta. His favorite color is green and he can be found at http://msmolarek.blogspot.com//

JAMES MATTHEWS
The Office

Matthew James Pullan, otherwise known as James Matthews, is a young writer who is from the suburbs of Manchester and loves to write to express his emotions. He has faced many traumas, such as battles against Cancer and depression so he doesn't fester around these topics. He writes and shares his pride and joy with you.

STEPHEN McQUIGGAN
Mr. Bitterbeans

Stephen McQuiggan was the original author of the bible; he vowed never to write again after the publishers removed the dinosaurs and the spectacular alien abduction ending from the final edit. His other, lesser known, novels are *A Pig's View Of Heaven* and *Trip A Dwarf*.

KATLYN MINARD
Death in a Hollywood Edit Bay

Katlyn Minard is an aspiring novelist whose short
fiction has appeared in *Capulet Magazine, Lunch Ticket, 101
Words,* and *Moon City Review.* She lives in Los Angeles.

INDEX

Printed in Great Britain
by Amazon